STARING DOWN THE DRAGON

DOROTHEA N. BUCKINGHAM

Staring Down The Dragon

Written by Dorothea N. Buckingham

Published by Sydney Press
Kaneohe, Hawaii 96744
Email: buckaloha@gmail.com
© Sydney Press

ISBN NO. 0-9724577-3-9

First Edition, Third Printing - 2022

Cover design: Sumanth Prabhaker
Book Design: Sumanth Prabhaker

ₚFor Charlie and Al

STARING DOWN THE DRAGON

Chapter One

He walked for fifteen minutes before
he thought he came to it.

"Cross it," she said, and he thought
there would be a bridge of some sort.

There was none.

—Toni Morrison, *Song of Solomon*

I didn't know what to wear my first day back at school. I wanted to look fantastic—better than fantastic—I wanted to look like I never had cancer. That was it. I *had* cancer, like I *had* a broken leg in seventh grade. Then my leg healed, like my cancer treatment was over, and I thought I could go back to school and be just me, Rell DeMello.

Enter memories: me in fifth grade, dancing hula in the Lei Day Pageant; me in seventh grade, captain of the soccer team; and me last September, at the beginning of my sophomore year, when I was diagnosed with cancer.

Before I was diagnosed, I never used the word cancer. Cancer was a disease old people got, and most of them died. But by April, I could do a science project on it, complete with myself as a visual aid.

When I was in treatment at Stanhope Hospital in San Francisco, I would dream about coming back home to Hawaii. I would dream about playing with my dog, about going to the beach, and driving around with my friend Emi. I made up scenes in my head about my first day back at Kailua High. I imagined kids would pile lei around my neck so high that you couldn't see my face. I imagined a "Welcome Home Rell" banner in big red letters. I even practiced a thank-you speech I'd give at my "Welcome Home Rell Assembly."

When the day came for me to go back to school, all I wanted to do was to sneak back to my old desk and pretend nothing had ever happened. Going back to school after being treated for cancer wasn't exactly like the first day after summer vacation. I didn't think any teacher would ask me to write an essay about what I did on my trip to Chemotherapy Village.

My mom told me I was going back to my regular class, but I was still afraid they'd put me in a special class, or assign me a special seat, like Ella Cunha, who wears two hearing aids and sits in the front row for every class. Most of all, I was afraid of kids' questions.

I knew I looked different. When I left Hawaii, I had long brown hair, with matching eyebrows and eyelashes, and a 34B chest. I was going back twenty pounds lighter, bald, wearing a wig, and sporting a six-inch pink scar across my neck that in no way could pass for bruises from heavy-duty kissing. All I needed were two bolts sticking out of my neck and I would have been shoo-in for the role of Frankenstein in any school play.

I was afraid. I was afraid that kids would stare at me. I was afraid they'd laugh. I was afraid they wouldn't talk to me. But most of all I was afraid of their questions.

On the Sunday night before I went back to school, I spent an hour in front of the mirror, practicing answering their questions. I smiled, I tilted my head, and I told jokes about myself. I made up stories about the cute doctors in the hospital, about riding the cable cars in San Francisco, and eating chocolate at Ghirardelli Square. I made it sound like a bad case of the flu.

When the day came to go back to school, my mother drove me—in her two-door, beige Saturn. She drove with two hands gripping the steering wheel, white-knuckled and in perfect silence until we pulled into the school parking lot. Then she said, "It's going to be okay." She said as if she were trying to convince both of us.

"I know, Mom," I answered.

"Really," she said, "it will be okay."

"Really, Mom, I know."

Then she drove in the parking lot, right through it and up to the front steps of school, right in front of packs of kids blasting their music, or getting their last grinding kisses in before the bell rang. I wanted to die. (Hmm, I almost did die, that's what got me in this mess to begin with.)

My mother rubbed my back. "I love you, Rell," she said it as if she had magical powers.

"I love you, too, Mom," I said.

I opened the door and inched out of the car. I slung my backpack over my shoulder and took my first step.

"Good luck, Sweetheart," Mom said.

I looked back. She waved at me and threw me a kiss like she was the Grand Marshal of the Mothers' Love Parade.

I told myself to smile, wave back, and watch her to make sure she drove away.

There it was: Kailua High School. I stared at all the kids jammed on the stairs. There were so many kids around. I felt like I was trapped in a fast-forward video, but I was in slow motion.

stared at the front door, hugged my backpack to my chest, and took the first step. I made it to the top of the steps—step-by-step and I stood there.

It's no big deal, I told myself. Just go in.

A guy shoved me and a herd of his buddies pushed past me. I was afraid that he would bump me and my scar would split open and my guts would spill out. It had been months since my surgery but I was still afraid someone would bump me. I imagined my guts leaking out on my shirt.

It's going to be okay, I told myself.

All I had to do was walk in the door. But I couldn't. I froze, then I turned around, I walked down the steps, took a right, and walked four blocks to McDonald's, where I spent the rest of the day.

That afternoon when my mom came to pick me up I was waiting at the sidewalk for her. When I got in the car, she leaned over and kissed me. "How did it go today, Sweetheart?" She stroked the back of my neck, careful not to touch my wig.

"It was great, Mom," I said with my best school-spirit smile plastered on my face.

"You look a little tired, Rell." She had one of her oh-my-poor-baby looks on her face.

I tossed my backpack on the floor. "A little," I said. "Not much."

"How about a little celebration for your first day back at school?"

My mother had to "celebrate" every step on my way back to recovery.

"We can stop at McDonald's," she said.

"No thanks," I said. The only thing I could get there was an order of super-sized trouble.

"We could go to Maui Taco or Jamba Juice," she said.

"I'm really not hungry, Mom."

"You need something in your stomach," she said.

If my mother couldn't kiss cancer away, she was going to feed it to death.

"No thanks," I said.

"Not even a shake?"

"No, Mom."

"You look tired."

"I'm not tired, Mom, and I'm not hungry." What I was, was scared to death that if she continued this conversation and didn't drive away, one of my friends would come out of school and run over to the car and ask me when I was coming back to school.

"I worry about you, Rell," she said.

I was worried about me, too, but not for the same reason.

Mom took off her sunglasses and fumbled through her purse. What could she possibly be looking for? The keys were in the ignition. What else could she need?

She angled the purse toward herself and pulled out a white envelope. "Some of the people from my department sent you a card." She handed me the card.

It's too bad Hallmark hasn't come out with an "I'm sorry you had cancer, glad to see you're still alive" card. They could make a fortune.

"I love you, Rell." Mom said.

I know you love me, but will you please just get out of here! I was thinking so loud, I was sure she could hear me. *Hurry.*

"Did you get to see your friends?" She shook her purse and dug deep inside.

What could she possibly be looking for?

"Uh-huh," I answered.

"Want a piece of gum?"

I shook my head.

"Rell, do you think you can catch up on your school work?"

I wanted to scream, "Drive!" but I said, "I think so. The hospital tutor was better than I thought." Since all I was doing was lying, why not throw in another one.

She started the car. Just then, Paul Cruz banged the hood of the car with his hand and waved. I waved back. Nate Lee was with him.

"Who's that?" she said as she put the car in gear.

"The genius who banged the car is Paul Cruz," I said.

"And the other guy?" She checked her rear view mirror and pulled away.

"Nate Lee," I said. "He's a junior."

"He's cute," she said.

"He's a junior, Mom," I said.

"Maybe he likes younger women." Mom smiled.

When my mother smiled, she was gorgeous. In real life, she was a forty-three-year-old college professor, but when she smiled, she looked like a college student—tall, thin, dark wavy hair and perfect olive skin that never had a zit.

I did inherit my mother's hair and skin, but my build was all my father's. "Athletic" is what the magazines called it. Of course, that was before my chemotherapy.

"Did you see Emi today?" she asked.

"We had lunch together." One more lie.

"And?" Mom wanted details so I gave her some.

"She met a new guy this weekend. He's some basketball player from St. Luke's." I named Emi's imaginary boyfriend Grant. I made him six-foot two-inches tall, one-hundred-eighty pounds, fair-skinned, with a mole on his left cheek.

"She's going to get him to ask her to their Spring Carnival, then she's going to dump him," I said.

"Do you have homework?" Mom asked.

"Not much."

"Did Mr. Owens talk to you?"

Mr. Owens was the school counselor.

"He told me he would give you a health room pass if you got tired," Mom said. He told me there's a cot in there where you could take a nap."

"When did he tell you that?" I asked.

"I went in to talk to him last week. Didn't he tell you?"

They talked last week. I was toast! My heart moved from my chest to my throat, and it was quickly working its way to my mouth.

"He was supposed to give you some paperwork that I have to mail to Stanhope."

I was dead meat.

"Rell." She looked over to me as she was driving. "Are you listening?"

Oh, yeah. I'm listening.

"Mr. Owens was out sick today." I hoped my lie was true.

Mom kept going with her questions. "Did you thank everyone for their cards?" she asked.

"Yup." I smiled. "I thanked everyone I saw."

But mainly I thanked the guy at McDonald's who kept filling my Coke and felt sorry for me when I told him I had cancer and I didn't go to school.

All the way home Mom asked me one question after another, and I gave her one good lie after another: Did you remember to pick up your form for your yearbook picture? Did you meet the exchange student from Brazil? Did you notice the new plumeria trees that the parents planted? And the big question, Did anyone say anything to upset you?

I was sick of questions. I craved a day with no questions—no questions, no charts, no poking, no prodding, no asking me about night sweats, fever, appetite loss or how my bowel movements were. I wanted one day when no one cared if I were hungry, tired, constipated, or dead.

I decided on asking her questions. Dad always said the best defense is a good offense.

"How was school for you?" I asked her.

"Terrific." She smiled. "Dr. Kosaki assigned me all online classes next semester, too. This way when we go back to Stanhope for your follow-up tests, or if anything happens, I can teach from there like I did this semester."

I knew I would be going back to Stanhope every six months for checkups, but I also knew what "if anything happens" meant. It meant if the cancer comes back.

I slouched down, crossed my arms, closed my eyes, and pretended to be asleep. It did not work. Mom kept talking.

"What about math class?" she asked. "You've always had trouble with math."

"Math class is okay," I said.

"Dad has an intern from the university working for him. He's an engineering student. I'm sure he could help you with your math."

Great. A geek engineer-wannabe who would spy for my father while he tutored me.

"I'll think about it," I said. Three more blocks and we would be home.

"You're not very strong in math, Rell."

I didn't answer. I kept my eyes closed until I felt us turn into our driveway and heard Mom turn off the engine.

"Just once I'd like the paper in the driveway instead of under the hedge." She sighed. Mom's an Olympic-caliber sigher.

"I'll get it," I said.

The paper was deep under the mock orange hedge. The ground around it was covered with wilted confetti petals that smelled so strong it was almost too sweet. I loved the smell of mock orange; it was one of the things I missed when I was in San Francisco.

When I was at Stanhope, a girl named LB was my best friend. She was a third-go-round patient. Sometimes, after her chemotherapy treatment, she thought her skin smelled like her chemo drugs, and she'd cry. That's when I told her about the smell of mock orange, and plumeria, and ginger. And when she said her food tasted like copper, I would tell her about the taste of huli-huli chicken, straight off the grill, smelling like *kiawe,* dripping with grease, and all dark from the smoke.

"Rell," Mom called. She was leaning against the front gate. She had her briefcase clutched under her arm. Her purse was dangling off her shoulder, and she had her books in the same hand she was trying to unlatch the gate with. "Could you bring in the mail, Sweetheart?"

"Sure," I said. I wished she'd stop calling me Sweetheart.

Mom opened the gate and out came Ajax. "Get down," Mom yelled at the dog. "Get down!" Of course, he jumped on her higher, then circled her legs, and sniffed at her skirt.

She kicked the gate closed and yelled at the dog. "Ajax, this nonsense has to stop. It has to stop." She repeated herself, slower and louder, emphasizing every syllable as if the dog was supposed to know that when she talked like that it meant that he was in big trouble.

I got the mail and followed Mom and Ajax into the house. I loved Ajax—he never asked me any questions. I squatted down and let him kiss my face. "Good boy," I said.

"Rell, do not let the dog…." She was hammering out the words just like she did to Ajax.

I knew the end of the sentence. "Do not let the dog lick your face" and I knew the right answer to give her. "Okay, Mom."

Before I could answer her, the phone rang. I was sure it was Mr. Owens. *I'm dead,* I thought. Dead Girl Walking. I dropped the mail on the kitchen counter and headed straight to my room. *Ten, nine, eight, seven.* I was mentally counting down to the Mom-explosion when she found out I skipped school.

"Rell." I heard my mother's voice. "That was Emi," she said. "She's on her way over."

I'm safe, I thought.

"You've got mail here, too," she said.

I came out to get it. My mail was *Seventeen* magazine.

Mom had already sorted the mail into piles: *Construction Engineering Monthly* for Dad, an English journal for herself, and a bill from Stanhope Hospital in Dad's pile.

"I'm going to bake cookies," she said. "What are you in the mood for? Oatmeal or chocolate chips?"

"Oatmeal," I answered, and grabbed my magazine and headed right back to my room, where I was still safe.

Who knows? Maybe Mr. Owens really was out for the day.

I plopped on my bed, took off my wig, and felt the cool air on my scalp. I tossed my wig on my dresser and accidentally caught a glimpse of myself in the mirror. There I was—a blue-skinned girl with a high-gloss scalp.

When I was five years old, I pulled out all the hair on my little Lizzie doll, leaving her with a scalp of empty holes and a few strands of black rayon. I could have passed for little Lizzie's big sister.

I leafed through *Seventeen* looking for bald-headed models with no eyebrows or eyelashes, but there were none. I craved hair.

Enter my fantasy: I'm running on the beach, barefoot, wearing a flowing white dress and my hair is billowing in the breeze.

Enter my reality: I lied on my bed wallowing in self-pity until my mother called out from the kitchen, "Emi's here."

I shot up, grabbed my wig, tugged it on, and straightened it out as quickly as I could. Emi had never seen me without it. Except for my parents, no one in Hawaii had.

Emi made a grand entrance into my room. "Just where were you today, Miss Rell?" She stood at my door. Her head was cocked, and her hands were on her hips.

"Shh!" I put my finger to my lips.

"Don't shush me," she said. "I just lied my head off to your mother about your great first day back at school." She lifted her eyebrows so high that they disappeared under her bangs. "Where were you?"

I grabbed her arm, pulled her into my room, and shut the door. "I wasn't at school."

"No fooling, Sherlock," Emi said. "The question was, 'Where were you?'"

"McDonald's," I said.

"McDonald's?" Emi repeated.

"Yeah," I said.

"All day?"

"Yup." I was finding it hard to believe it myself.

"Was it the hot guys or the cold food?" Emi asked.

"There was only one hot guy," I said. "His name is Gus. He's seventy. He's got bad breath, walks with a cane, and drives a red Miata convertible."

"Cute," Emi said and she stretched out on my bed. "Seriously, where'd you go?"

"Seriously, I was at McDonald's."

"Why?"

"I didn't want to go back to school," I said.

"And you couldn't think of anything better to do?"

"Okay, it wasn't the greatest place to hang out, but I've been sick, remember? My brain's slow."

"Right, you had cancer and now you have dreams about Ronald McD and his golden arches."

"I just couldn't face going back," I said. "When I got out of the car, and saw all those kids." I shrugged. "It felt like they were all staring at me and...." Tears dripped out of my eyes.

"You okay?" Emi asked.

"What do you think?" I twisted my mouth into a half-smile.

"Dumb question," she said.

Emi was my best friend. We met in third grade. We played on

the same soccer team, we quit Girl Scouts on the same day (our first day), and every Fourth of July I went camping with her family.

"What if, tomorrow morning, I came by and picked you up?" she said. "Then we can walk into school together."

"I don't think so," I said.

"I could pick up Sarah on the way."

I shook my head.

"The two of us could throw rose petals at your feet as you walk in." Emi was trying to cheer me up, but she was only making things worse.

"Not in the plan," I said.

"What if we got Jonathan Akana to chant you in? Imagine. Jonathan Akana in a skimpy *malo,* blowing a conch shell and the wind blowing." Emi wiggled her eyebrows. "The *malo* flies higher."

"Enough," I said.

"Come on, Rell. You need something to snap you out of it."

"I'm fine," I said.

"Right. I noticed how fine you are," she said.

I didn't answer.

Emi stood up and looked in the mirror. Of the two of us (Emi) was the pretty one—I was the smart one. I was also the short one, the one with the round dark eyes and the 34B chest (at least I used to have a chest before treatment). Emi was half-Japanese and half-Hawaiian, tall, lean, with great long hair, and teardrop onyx eyes that disappeared when she smiled.

"Wait, I've got it," she said. "We'll go shopping."

"I hate shopping, remember?" It was Emi who was the mall diva.

"Island Girls is having a close out sale," she said. "They've got boa feather earrings for seventy-five percent off."

"They should be giving them away," I said.

"All the movie stars are wearing them," she said.

Besides being a mall diva, Emi was a movie star magazine

junkie. She knew everything every celebrity was wearing, what they ate for breakfast, who they were dating, who they were cheating on. She bought everything they did—just a cheaper version.

Emi pulled her keys out of her purse, and jingled them in the air. "We could go to my house after the mall," she said. "No one's home."

"No one?"

"No one."

"Okay," I said, and I gave her a thumbs up.

CHAPTER TWO

M om," I yelled, "can I go to Emi's house?"

"And to the mall?" Emi added.

I turned to Emi. "No mall."

"Yes, mall," she said.

"I can't hear you," Mom yelled back from the kitchen.

"Emi, I really, really don't want to go to the mall," I said.

"Rell, come on. Just five seconds in Island Girls."

Mom knocked on my door.

"Come in," I said, then turned to Emi and mouthed the words "No mall."

Mom wiped the flour off her hands on to a kitchen towel. "The cookies will be ready in a few minutes," she said. "Now, what did you say? I couldn't hear you."

"Mom, could I go to—"

"The mall," Emi finished my sentence.

Mom looked at me. She sighed yet one more of her heave-up-the-world sighs. "Estrella," she said, "after being at school all day, do you think you should be with more people?"

Those were the words she said, but what she really meant was, "If you go to the mall, a kid with the measles, mumps, or Bubonic Plague will sneeze on you and you will almost die, and, on the way to the hospital, an alien, in the form of an emergency medical worker, will inject you with a glowing green serum and kidnap you to Planet 53."

"We're just going to Island Girls to get some lipstick, Mrs. De-Mello. Then we're going straight to my house," Emi said.

"Mom, I'm *not* going to the mall. I promise. I'll stay in the car," I said.

"Okay," she gave in. "But be careful."

I went to the bathroom to straighten out my wig and tried to draw eyebrows on myself. The eyebrows were the thing. Once they went, it was like a neon sign: WARNING: CANCER KID.

"Hurry up," Emi called.

"Give me a minute." I wiped off the eyebrows and tried again. That time I looked like an angry smiley-face, so I gave up, tugged my wig down one more time, and when I opened the door, there was Emi playing with my Hat-Hair wig. It was a cap with two separate wigs. The one under the visor made bangs.

"This is neat," she said. She pulled the bangs off the Velcro strip.

"Yeah, the wig in the back comes off, too." I flipped it over for her "It's so you can get long or medium hair if you want it and still keep the bangs the same."

"Do they sell ponytails?" she asked.

"I guess," I said, "but then the sides of your scalp would show and you'd still look bald."

"Cool," Emi said and balanced the Hat-Hair wig over my lamp-shade. "You should draw a face on the shade and name her 'Hattie.'"

"You're warped."

"And proud of it," Emi said.

I grabbed my *Seventeen* magazine and we were off. I hated the mall. I hated it before I got sick and I hated it more after. To be honest, Mom wasn't the only one who was afraid of all those sneezing snot-nosed kids and their nasty germs. I was afraid of them, too. And—insert drum roll here—I didn't want to be stared at by every jerk who was freaked out by a girl wearing a wig and having a face with no eyebrows.

I got in Emi's car, pulled down the visor, and straightened my wig again. I counted my eyelashes. I had five wispy, wimpy hairs, but they were all mine, and soon there would be more.

Emi started the car. "You ready, Miss Rell?"

"I am, Miss Em."

She looked back as she pulled out of the driveway. "You missed big news at school today," she said.

"The gossip gods must be punishing me," I said.

"During first period chemistry Rhonda announced that Stacey Liu is pregnant."

"Wow! Is it Darren's?"

"You would think," Emi said. "But macho-man Darren went around all morning saying, 'It's not mine.'"

"What a jerk."

"No," Emi said, "it's the truth." She snickered. "Get this. At lunchtime big-deal-I-know-all-about-sex-Stacey admitted she and Darren never had sex."

"All those camping trips on the North Shore?"

"Separate sleeping bags, and Stacey's sister went with them most of the time."

"In the same tent?" I asked.

"Same tent."

"I don't believe it," I said.

"It gets better." Emi turned to me. "She never had sex with anybody! She told Wanda, who told Kim. Then Kim told Wanda and it was a CNN news flash."

"And all this time I thought I was the world's oldest virgin," I said.

"I'm three months older than you, remember? I've got that title," Emi said.

The light turned red at the intersection by the fire station. Emi pointed to a few bare-chested firefighters who were washing down their truck.

"I betcha they're hot," she said, grinning.

I groaned.

"I betcha if you walked into school with one of them on your arm everyone would notice," Emi said.

She didn't get it. I didn't want to be noticed. I wanted to be invisible.

"I wish I could transfer to another school," I said.

"Why? It'll be great going back, Rell. Lots of kids ask about you."

"That's what I'm afraid of." I looked at my reflection in the car window. "I look like a baby bird in a cheap-ass wig."

"It's an expensive-ass wig. Your father told me so." Emi lowered her voice to mimic my dad's. "Nothing but the best for my Estrella. Only the best."

"I even got the best cancer," I said.

"You don't have the best cancer," Emi corrected me. "You have a good cancer."

She was right. I had Hodgkin's disease; it was a "good cancer." As if it were a cancer that behaved well in school, and did all its homework. It was a good cancer—it only killed the worst of its cases.

I hunched my shoulders and made my voice warble like the lady at church who'd said, "Lucky you, Rell. Hodgkin's disease is a good cancer to have."

"But it is," Emi said.

"I'd rather lie down on the street and get hit by an ice cream truck, thank you very much."

"Stop it, Rell."

"At least that way I could die with an Eskimo Pie smashed in my face."

"It's over, Rell. Move on."

It's never over—that was the point she never understood.

I knew Hodgkin's was a good cancer. Some of the doctors actually use the word "cured" when they talk about their patients. When I heard that, it made me feel guilty. There I was, surrounded by kids with amputated legs or not such great odds of staying alive and I had an easy cancer, a good cancer like Hodgkin's. Lucky me.

Emi pulled into the mall parking lot near Island Girls. She pulled down the rear view mirror, put on some lipstick, and pulled her hair into a big clip.

Emi glossed her lips fifteen million times a day, and she combed her hair two million times. I hardly ever wore makeup. I rarely wore jewelry, and the sexiest outfit I had was a clean T-shirt and jeans.

"Let's go," she said.

"I'm not going," I said.

"In and out. I swear." She crossed her heart with her fingers.

"I can't."

"Once around the mall." She clasped her hands in prayer. "Come on."

"No." I shook my head.

"Is it because of the cheap-ass wig?" she asked.

"Something like that."

"Okay," Emi said. "But next time you're coming in."

Emi kept the keys in the ignition and turned on the radio. "I'll be right out," she said. "Five minutes. Time me."

"Emi," I said. "Wait." I flipped my *Seventeen* magazine to an article about makeup makeovers. "Do you think you could pick up some stuff to make me look like this?" I showed her the picture of the Natural Beauty model.

"Sure," she said. "No worries."

I knew I should worry.

Emi dashed across the parking lot into the mall. I watched as her glimmering black hair swung in the sunlight and wished I could have hair like that. *Glimmering black hair swinging in the sunlight.* Who talks like that? I asked myself.

Bald girls was my answer.

"Honolulu City Lights" was playing on the oldies station. I loved the part in that song about the guy leaving Hawaii and seeing the Honolulu city lights from the plane. Then he lifts his *pikake* lei to his nose and smells it.

I thought about LB, and how she loved the *pikake* lei my mother gave her. She kept calling it jasmine and showed it off to all the nurses.

I sang along with "Honolulu City Lights," and with the next four songs that played. My eyes were fixed on the mall entrance. I started to count the number of people coming out. I was at twenty-three and there was still no sign of Emi. It was getting hot in the car. I kept counting. Thirty-one people came out of the mall, but still no Emi. I knew I'd have to go in and get her.

But what if someone sees me? I thought. *Well, so what if they do?* I answered myself. I argued with myself, playing back the words of the hospital psychologist: "No one can make you feel uncomfortable. Only you can make yourself feel uncomfortable." *That's such crap.*

Of course, people can make you feel ashamed. I remember in eighth grade when I dove in the pool at school and my bathing suit top rolled down to my waist. It was all over school in minutes. Of course I was ashamed.

By that time, I had had it with waiting for Emi. I was going to go in and get her. I got out of the car, squared my shoulders, and walked across the parking lot. I was halfway across when I heard someone call my name. "Rell?"

A Dodge pickup truck with tinted windows pulled over to the curb.

"Rell is that you?"

It was Nate Lee.

I thought, *If I'd only waited thirty more seconds before getting out of the car, no one would have seen me.* Well, maybe that's not true.

Do the math, Rell.

You live on an island.

Everyone goes to the mall.

Someone was going to see you.

"Hi, Nate." I waved to him with one hand and held on to my wig with the other. "I'm late." I pointed to the mall. "I'm meeting Emi," I said and ran to the automatic door entrance.

Nate leaned out the window. "You're looking good, Rell," he said.

The automatic doors took forever to open. I was sure Nate was staring at me, standing there, holding my wig, praying to disappear.

When the doors closed behind me, I felt safe. I found Emi at the Island Girls at the checkout counter.

"Look." She opened a bag filled with bronzers, brushed, mascaras, and three lipsticks. "It's all for your 'Extreme Makeover,' Rell."

I knew it was a mistake to ask her to do my makeup.

"When I'm through with you, you're going to be drop-dead gorgeous," she said.

She could have used a better choice of words.

"Check this out." Emi held up a pot of blue glitter.

"No."

"Wait!" She dragged me over to the rack of false eyelashes. "What do you think?" She held them up to her eyes.

"No."

"You're going to love them." She handed the eyelashes to the cashier who added them to the pile.

"Emi, I said no."

I said no all the way back, and was still saying no as I sat on the chair in front of her bedroom dresser.

"Emi, I will not wear false eyelashes."

She popped open the box and put one up to her eye and blinked.

"Not in a thousand years."

"They would make such a big difference," Emi pleaded.

"I'd look like the waitress at Flamingo's," I said.

"You mean Iris, with the lace handkerchief pinned under her name tag?"

"That would be the one," I said.

"Iris would be so proud of you, Rell."

"There's nothing to glue them on to," I said. "I've got five eyelashes, I counted them. What if you glue one of those strips too close to my real lashes and when I peel it off it takes my good ones with it?"

Emi put the lashes on her dresser. "Okay, you've got a point." Before I could exhale she said, "But there's always Halloween."

I counted on my fingers. "May, June, July, August, September, October. Five months," I said. "We'll see."

Emi emptied the bag of makeup on her dresser. "Let's get started." She lined up what she bought then went to her bathroom to get more. While she was in there I told her I saw Nate Lee in the parking lot.

"What did he say?" she asked. Emi was sitting on the floor in front of her bathroom sink, rooting around, pulling out lotions and creams and bottles of who knows what.

"Hi," I answered.

"Hi yourself," Emi said.

"No. That's what Nate Lee said. He said hi."

"That was profound." She stood up cradling all of her potions. "Did he have anything else to say? He's never without an opinion."

"He said quote, 'You're looking good, Rell.'"

Emi dumped the stuff on her dresser. "Who does he think he is telling you you're looking good?"

"I don't know," I said. "I thought it was kind of sweet. He *is* a junior."

"Nate Lee is sooo California." Emi opened three bottles of foundations

"I didn't know he was from California. I thought he transferred from St. Luke's."

"He did." She put three stripes of foundation on my jaw line then checked the colors in the mirror.

"He's got a nice truck," I said.

"If you like rust and Bondo." Emi dabbed the foundation on my forehead and ran her fingers over my forehead under my wig. "Rell, would you mind taking off your wig?"

It was a big question. She had never seen me bald. What if she couldn't handle it, I thought. What if she made one of those oh-my-God faces and went screaming out of the room?

Such drama.

"It would be a lot easier to put the makeup on," Emi said.

Easier for her, maybe, but this wasn't so easy for me. Here it goes, I thought. I slipped my hands under the wig's elastic and lifted it off my head. I lifted my head, but I couldn't look at her. "Is this what you thought I'd look like?" I asked.

"Pretty much," she said. "No big deal."

I tried not to look at myself in the mirror. I looked at the posters of all the movie stars on Emi's walls, the University of Hawaii pennant, the photos of me, Sara, and Emi that were shoved in her mirror frame. I looked at her stuffed animals, at the layer of dust on her dresser, at the floating specks caught in the sun. I looked at everything and everywhere except at my face in the mirror.

"Emi, can you work without me looking in the mirror?" I asked.

"Sure," she said. So I swiveled around.

Emi picked up a sponge and held it high. "Are you ready to be beautiful, Miss Rell?"

"I am," I said, but I didn't believe in miracles.

Emi angled my chin to the ceiling. "Look up." She dipped the sponge in the foundation.

"Is Nate Lee originally from California?" I asked.

"No, Kaimuki," Emi said. "He just goes there a lot. While you were at Stanhope he went to San Francisco twice." She patted a sponge under my eye. "He had some family thing going on. I heard his grandfather was dying."

"Oh," I said but with my chin pointed up, it sounded more like a grunt.

"Yeah. He took off from school a week the last time he went to the mainland." Emi stroked the makeup over my jaw line and neck. I'm surprised Wanda didn't start a rumor that you two were secretly meeting in San Francisco," Emi said.

I clutched at Emi's arm and with great drama I said, "Emi, I've been lying to you all this time. I never had cancer. Nate and I would meet in Las Vegas. We were married in an Elvis chapel, but I didn't want to tell you I'm not a virgin anymore."

She yanked my jaw to the left. "Don't talk stupid when I'm trying to work on your face."

"You're just jealous," I said.

"Jealous of you and Nate Lee? I don't think so." She swirled a brush into the pot of blush and shook the excess into her hand.

"He talked to me once at the beginning of the year," I said.

Emi turned on the radio.

"I don't care what you think. I think he's cute," I said.

She turned up the volume on the radio. "I can't hear you," she said and went back to working on my face. "Make a long O with your mouth," she ordered.

I stretched out my mouth and she poked at it with a lip brush. It made my nose tingle.

"Now pout," she said.

I pouted.

"Not like that," Emi said. "No. Soft, like just before a kiss." She angled my chin higher up. "Pout again," she said.

I pouted again and that time I got it right.

I tried talking to her while she worked, but each time I started to say anything, she told me not to move, so I sat there and listened to the radio and Emi's tone-deaf singing. She worked on me for almost half an hour before she declared me done.

She stepped back and looked at me. She picked up the *Seventeen* magazine and held up the page next to my face, then she looked at me again. "Voila!" she said. "Take a look."

I turned around and looked in the mirror. "Oh, my God! I look like a porn queen," I said. "A bald porn queen."

"Rell, I know it's a little more makeup then you're used to."

"Emi...." I was speechless.

Just then, the front door to her house slammed open. "Emi, could you pull your car in?" It was Emi's brother Kalani.

"Be right there," she yelled to him, then turned to me. "Give it a few minutes. Maybe it is a lot of color."

"Maybe?"

"But I did a great job, didn't I?" Emi held up the photo in the magazine. On page 173 there was the "Makeup for the Natural Beauty." On page 174 there was "The Vamp of the Night Look."

"You got the wrong page," I said.

"The other page is so boring," Emi said. "What I did is more of a blend. You know, 'fusion' style."

"Emi! Now!" Kalani yelled again.

"It said I'll be right there," she answered him. "Just give it a second," she said to me. "We can make adjustments."

When she got back, I held up my hands to show her that they were caked with iridescent mauve.

"It was too much, huh?" Emi asked.

"Okay," she said.

"I want the 'boring' makeup," I said.

"A perfect match for you," Emi said.

"And I'm going to watch you this time."

Not only did I watch her, but also I took notes on how she lightened the dark circles under my eyes, and drew in real-looking eyebrows. I took notes as she explained how to swirl the brush in the concealer powder and blend it to look natural. With each step, a more normal-looking girl emerged. When Emi was finished, a healthy-looking girl appeared in the mirror.

"What do you think now?" Emi asked.

"You're a genius."

"I know." She blew on her fingernails and brushed them against her chest.

And, of course, we hugged.

"What about tomorrow?" Emi asked. "You want me to come over to your house before school and do it again?"

"I think I can do it." I held up my notes. "If not I'll call you."

I hugged her again. "Going to school's going to be so much easier, Em."

"I still think you could use more color," Emi said.

I didn't even answer her. "Emi, wait until my mother sees me. She's been trying to get to wear more makeup ever since we got back from California. She's going to love it!"

"Just a little more eye shadow and some glitter on your cheeks," she said.

"No more nothing," I said.

While Emi drove me home, she went over the makeup directions one more time.

"I got it," I said. When we got to my house, I ran inside. Ajax was at the door, wagging his tail and sniffing at my feet. I was sniffing too—homemade oatmeal cookies.

I could hear CNN on in the family room. In our house, the family room and the kitchen were one big room. I could see my mother. She was hunkered down on the couch, surrounded by student papers, journals, a coffee mug, and the TV remote.

I took a bite of a cookie. "Great cookies, Mom," I said and shared the rest with Ajax. "I've got a surprise for you," I said. "Close your eyes."

I walked into the family room and stood in front of her. *Wait until she sees me. She's going to love it.*

"Okay," I said. "Open your eyes." I spun around in front of her and took a bow.

She didn't smile and beam and gush all over me. Instead, she slid her eyeglasses down her nose and looked at me from above them. She wasn't smiling.

"Mr. Owens called me," she said. "He wanted to know why you weren't in school today."

Chapter Three

I figured I would be grounded forever—no phone calls and no TV. It was another milestone on my road to recovery—my first punishment since I got sick.

"Do you have anything to say?" Mom asked. Her voice was calm. It would have been better if she were yelling.

I shook my head.

I glanced over at the TV. CNN was doing a story on the Marine Corps' new boot camp.

"Rell, we need to talk." She patted the sofa cushion, and as soon as she did, Ajax leaped up next to her.

"Get down!" She pointed to the floor.

Poor dog, I thought. He must be so confused.

"Sit, Rell."

And like a good dog, I sat.

"Rell, I know this has been a tough year on you," she said.

I glanced at the TV and wished I were at the Marine Corps boot camp. I'd rather face a drill sergeant than my mother.

"It's been tough on all of us," she said.

I nodded.

"Your going back to school was something we were all looking forward to." She had a crumpled tissue clutched in her fist

I looked at the TV again. Marines were hanging on a rope that was dangling from flying helicopter.

Mom turned off the TV. "Rell…." she said.

"…I'm sorry, Mom."

"Let me talk." She put her hand up like a crossing guard stopping traffic. "Rell, I was worried about you all day long. I was glued to my pager. I checked my voice mail every ten minutes and dropped by the office twice to see if you had called." She took in a deep breath. "But, when you didn't call, I thought things were okay. And when I picked you up from school, you seemed happy." She shook her head. "All day I was worried sick, but then—you were okay." Her eyes were red and her mascara was gone. "Where were you, Rell?"

I told her the truth. "I went to McDonald's."

"McDonald's?"

Every time I said it, I knew how dumb it sounded.

Mom combed her fingers through her hair and pulled it in a bunch at the back of her neck. "You spent the whole day at Mc-Donald's?"

"Yes."

"Was Emi with you?"

"She didn't know anything about it." I reached down to pet the dog. "I know it looks bad, but it was really no big deal."

"It is a big deal, Rell."

Only if you make it one, Mom.

"Rell, this kind of behavior isn't normal for you. If you weren't ready to go back to school, you should have told us." She sighed. "You know Dad and I would have understood. We could have put it off for another week. My God, Rell, we could have talked to Mr. Owens about you being home schooled for the rest of the year."

"I don't want to be home schooled," I said. "I'm ready to go back. I just…I just couldn't do it today."

"Rell, it's more serious than you think."

"No it's not, Mom! It's not like I killed somebody or robbed a bank." I could feel the tears building up in my eyes.

"Rell."

"I will go to school tomorrow. You can walk me in if you want to. I don't care."

"But why didn't you go today?"

"I don't know why."

The phone rang.

"Rell, there's more to this."

"No, there's not, Mom." I could hear my voice crack. "Why do you have to turn everything into a soap opera?"

"Rell, you need to deal with this."

The phone kept ringing.

"There's nothing to deal with, Mom. I got scared, that's it. It's over."

On the fifth ring, Mom picked up the phone. "Hello." She looked up at me and gave me a this-isn't-over-young-lady look. "No, David, she's fine. She just got home."

Dad was on the phone.

"She was at Emi's house." Mom walked into the kitchen. "Why bother getting involved now?" she said.

I could tell a fight was brewing.

"I'll call," Mom said. "What's the number?" She flipped through the notes clipped to the refrigerator door. "I've got it," she said. "Right here." Then there was a pause.

"Don't make promises you can't keep, David," she said. "No, that's fine. No, it's fine. Rell and I will go out for dinner." Another pause. "I told you David, I don't care."

It was another fight.

Mom paced between the sink and the fridge with the phone nuzzled against her shoulder. "I said fine, David." And she hung up—no "I love you," or "I'll see you later tonight,' not even a good-bye, just a "Fine."

Mom turned to me. "Dad's going to work late."

"I figured," I said.

"We can go out to eat, or…" She opened the refrigerator, and moved things around. "…have left over stir fry."

"Do we have any frozen pizza?"

She opened the freezer. "You're in luck." She held up a box of pizza. "Sausage and mushroom."

"Great," I said.

"Rell." Mom's voice got serious again.

I didn't let her finish. "I'm sorry about missing school," I said.

"Rell, sometimes I don't think I can handle one more thing, Sweetheart."

"Me neither, Mom. That's why I didn't go to school." I looked at her.

"What's this?" she said and cupped my chin in her hands. "Makeup?"

"Emi did it. It was the big surprise I made you close your eyes for."

"You look beautiful."

I pulled out the *Seventeen* magazine and opened it to the "Natural Beauty" picture.

"She did a great job," Mom said. "And these notes?" She angled the magazine to read my notes in the margin.

"Emi taught me how to do it, so when I go to school tomorrow, I can do it myself."

"Rell, I still want you to talk to Dr. Maitlin about not going to school."

Dr. Maitlin was my psychologist.

"I don't need to talk to her," I said.

"Just this time, Rell, for me. You need to discuss this issue."

"There is no issue, Mom."

"Just this time, Rell."

It was always "just this time."

"Why don't you talk to her?" I said.

"I can't. I'm swamped at school right now, Rell."

"Why don't' you talk to her about you and Dad?"

"Dad and I are not the issue."

"The two of you fight all the time."

"Rell, I already made an appointment for you. She can see you on Thursday."

"Can't I just call her instead?"

When I was at Stanhope I called Dr. Maitlin every week. I had a hospital psychologist there, but I liked Dr. Maitlin better. She never lied to me and she never told Mom what I said.

"I'll pick you up after school on Thursday," Mom said.

It was a done deal. I was going to Dr. Maitlin's.

When I was a little kid and my mother was cold, I would have to put on a sweater. When she was tired, I had to take a nap. Now, when she got upset, I was the one who had to see the psychologist.

"Fine," I said.

I didn't have a choice.

That night when Mom tucked me in bed, she ran her hand over my forehead. "I'm sorry I got so worried about you, Sweetheart. But I love you, Rell."

"I love you, too, Mom."

Then she got up and stopped at the door to throw me a kiss.

I listened to hear her footsteps echo down the hall. When I was sure she was in the kitchen, I patted my hand on the bed, and Ajax jumped up. He pawed at my quilt, circled around twice, and coiled himself snugly against my back. Within minutes, the dog was snoring, but I couldn't get to sleep.

I watched Ajax run in his sleep. His paws fluttered and he was making muffled barking sounds. At nine forty-five, I heard Dad come home. The minute he walked in the door, he and Mom started fighting. An hour later, they were still fighting.

It was after midnight when they stopped and I finally fell asleep. I had a dream that I was stuck at the top of a Ferris wheel. My hands are clenched on the bar. The gondola rocks faster and faster. I scream. The cotton candy man looks up at me. He stares at me and grins.

I hated that nightmare. When I was in treatment, I had it all the time, but that was the first time I had it since I was at home. I reached over and hugged Ajax, and I tried to stay awake so I wouldn't have the nightmare again. I got up, stuffed a towel under my door, and turned on my computer. There was mail from LB. The subject line was: "Just found these."

They were photos of LB and me and Tess at the Halloween Party. There was one picture of Dr. Braden dressed like Elvis. The nurses were dressed like his 1950s teenagers. That was about a month before Tess died.

When I saw Tess's face, I remembered the first time we met. She was sitting in her wheelchair. There were Mylar ribbons braided through the spokes of its wheels. Tess was my first roommate at Stanhope. She had bone cancer—she donated her left leg to it. I'm not sure if I would have liked Tess if she didn't have cancer. She bordered on weird. She wore a curly red wig with a blue sequin cap, and when she talked, she waved a glittery crescent moon wand that dropped metal flakes all over the floor, the sheets, my chair, my pillow, and me.

A few weeks before she died, I heard her sobbing in the middle of the night. I pretended to be asleep.

"Rell, are you awake?" she whispered from across the street.

I groaned.

"Do you think butterflies would like flying around in the snow?"

"It's late, Tess," I answered.

"What if they knew they would die if they did it? Do you think they still would?

"I don't know, Tess."

"Rell, I want to fly."

A week after that conversation, her doctor told her that her treatment wasn't working. They called in her parents for a big conference with a whole team of doctors to discuss what the "options" were. After her parents left, I went back into our room. Her curly red wig was stuffed in the garbage can, and the glitter moon wand was broken in two.

"My doctors want me to try another experimental treatment," she said. "It'll be my fourth clinical trial."

I sat next to her on her bed and held her hand. It was fifteen minutes before she spoke again. Then she looked at me and said, "No more."

During the next few weeks, she lost a lot of weight. Her voice got softer, and she stopped wearing tie-dyed scarves.

One night she whispered to me from her bed. "I'm going to fold myself up like a butterfly and fly away."

A week later she was dead.

Mom didn't go to Tess's funeral. She had to go back to Hawaii that week. So, Dr. Braden drove LB and me to the funeral. On the walk up to the gravesite, he put his arm around LB and he held my hand.

It was the first time in my life I really knew someone who died, and it was only the second time I went to a funeral. I didn't know how to act. I knew how to act when I went to church, or went to see a play, but when it came to a friend's funeral, I didn't know what to do.

Dr. Braden walked LB and me to the reserved wooden seats under the canopy. I was sure everybody was staring at me, wondering if I was going to die next. I tried not thinking about dying. I thought about how the ground reeked of horse-manure fertilizer, and how I didn't want it to rain because I would have to trudge through manure puddles to get back to the car. Then Tess's mom sat down in the front row. Tess's dad had to help hold her up. She sat there, staring at Tess's coffin, and I remembered how, when I first got diagnosed, I thought I was going to die. I remembered how sorry I felt for my parents, and how sad they would be when I died, and how I felt like I had done something bad by getting sick.

I printed out the photo of Tess, taped it to my computer monitor, and went back to bed. It was three a.m; in four hours my alarm would go off to get me up to go to school. I snuggled under the covers, next to Ajax. He was stretched out, then he raised his head, looked at me, yawned, and went back to sleep. It must be great to be a dog.

When the alarm went off, I dragged myself into the shower, not really totally awake. I turned on the water, soaped up my washcloth, and slid it down my chest and stomach, careful not to touch my scar.

I ran the cloth over my scalp. A few more weeks, I thought, and I'll be ready for shampoo.

"It's quarter after seven," Mom yelled.

"I know, Mom." I dried myself off, got dressed, and propped the *Seventeen* up behind the sink. I followed Emi's directions exactly. I heard her voice in my head, "Swirl and flick," she said. "Bring the color to your eyes, not your nose. Stroke. Flick. Blend. Gloss."

"It's seven-thirty," Mom announced.

I stepped back to get a better view of my face in the mirror. "Not bad," I said. "Not bad at all."

By the time I came out for breakfast, Dad had already left for work. He was leaving earlier and coming home later and later. I ate my breakfast, careful not to say or do anything that would upset my mother. When she was ready to leave, I picked up my backpack and followed her to the car.

The "Kit and Kimo Show" was on the car radio. Life seemed normal. Their jokes were still bad, and their weather report was the same.

I asked Mom if she would let me off in the school parking lot and not drive up to the front of school, and she agreed.

"Do you have your cell phone with you, Rell?"

"Yes, Mom. It's permanently attached to me."

"Do you have my pager number?"

"The same one you've had for three years, Mom?"

"I'll be in the computer lab most of the day," she said. "Page me if you need me. I can leave anytime."

"I know, Mom."

She leaned over and gave me a hug. "I love you, Sweetheart."

"Me, too, Mom." I got out of the car. "You don't have to stick around," I said. "I really am going in."

"I love you, Rell."

"Bye, Mom."

She waved but didn't pull away. I could feel here eyes on me as I was walking away.

I went in the door. One small step for me, one giant leap into the unknown.

Step One: Go to Mr. Owens's office.

Mr. Owens was about forty years old, overweight, slightly balding, with dyed black hair and yellow teeth. He had a thick neck and a square jaw. In college he was an athlete. His shelves were crammed with peeling gold football trophies, but very few books. On the wall, right next to his college diploma, was a framed certificate for completing the Tinman Triathlon ten years ago.

He asked me to take a seat, and I did and I sat up like a good little girl.

"Today will be an adjustment for you, Estrella." He sounded like he'd practiced that line all morning.

"Yes, it will," I said.

"You know, there are stages of accepting changes in life," he said. "Changes like," he cleared his throat, "having an illness."

I stared at the spray can of Raid and the line of ant hotels on his windowsill.

"Umm…these changes include anger, resentment, and rebellion," he said.

His office smelled like popcorn.

"Has anyone talked to you about these stages, Estrella?"

I nodded.

"It's normal to rebel during these stressful times and do things you might not ordinarily do. Like cutting school yesterday, for example." He smiled.

There were burnt popcorn kernels on his desk. There was probably popcorn on the floor under his desk. No wonder he had ants and roaches.

"You may be going through a rebellion period now." He picked up a manila folder on his desk and fidgeted with it.

I watched a line of ants march up the wall behind his desk and out the window, right past the ant hotels and the can of Raid.

"You may be experiencing a post-traumatic period in your life."

I wanted to say I wasn't experiencing any periods since my chemotherapy, and the doctors weren't sure I would ever be able to get pregnant, but I thought if I did, it would probably give him a present-traumatic shock.

"Students may be curious about your appearance." He kept playing with the manila folder. "You do look different. You have lost a considerable amount of weight."

And I'm wearing a wig. But doesn't my makeup look great?

"They may ask you questions," Mr. Owens said.

Like, What's the capital of North Dakota? That's always been a hard one for me.

"If you would like me to, I could schedule a sensitivity session in each of your classes," he said.

"No thanks," I said, wondering if it was Bismark or Helena that was the capital.

"If you change your mind, let me know," he said.

I was beginning to feel sorry for the guy. Here he was, having to talk to a girl straight out of the cancer ward. It probably wasn't his favorite thing to do. I wondered what his favorite thing to do was, and decided it was giving locker room talks to the boys about how to wear condoms.

Finally, Mr. Owens gave me an envelope of papers that I needed to give Mom. Then he stood up, shook my hand, and wished me luck. It was almost funny.

I shook his hand, swung my backpack over my shoulder, and headed down to English class. Classes had already started, the hallway was empty, and I began to run. I don't know why I ran—if I was running from Mr. Owens, or running to get to class, or just plain running. When I opened the door to class, I was still panting. Mr. Meyers stopped lecturing and everyone in the room got quiet and still.

Chapter Four

Welcome back, Rell," Mr. Meyers said.

"Thanks," I said.

I started down the row of desk into the empty one that was mine when Mr. Meyers called me to the front of the class. He extended his arm out to me. "This is a big day for us," he said.

As I edged over to him, Frank Vasconsales and Faye Shibuya got out of their seats. They each had a lei in their hand.

"Welcome back, Rell." Faye draped a ti-leaf and pink-rose lei over my shoulders; she kissed me and gave me a big hug.

Frank shuffled up behind her. "Yeah, Rell," he said. "We missed you." He practically tossed the tuberose lei over my head.

Somebody from the back of the room yelled out. "Way to go, Frank."

I held the tuberose up to my nose and inhaled it.

"It looked a lot better yesterday," Frank said.

The petals were a bit brown.

"Thanks." I stood on my tiptoes and kissed his cheeks, and that started a chorus of whistles and catcalls.

"You gonna kiss me like that, Rell?" Paul Cruz yelled out.

"Anytime, cuz," I said and I laughed. *I laughed!* It was my first day back and it wasn't so bad.

"I missed you, Rell," Paul said.

"Thanks, Paul."

He stood up and took a deep bow.

"Sit down, Stud Man," Carole said. "Let her be."

"Thanks, everybody," I said and I laughed.

Paul Cruz started a chant. "Rell. Rell. Rell. Rell." And one by one the whole class stood up, and chanted, and clapped. They were clapping for me, like it was a movie, starring me, Rell DeMello.

"We are all happy to have you back," Mr. Meyers said and the class clapped again.

This was better than any lame daydream about a banner and a "Welcome Home Rell" assembly. The kids in my class were truly happy I was back.

"Thanks," I said. "Thanks, a lot."

When everyone settled down, Mr. Meyers scanned the room, and then pointed to Leilani. "If you need some help catching up on things, Leilani volunteered to tutor you."

Leilani waved at me and threw a kiss.

"And Wanda." Mr. Meyers pointed to where she was sitting. "Wanda kept a journal of what happened in class while you were gone."

"Waa-nn-dahh," some boy sang out. "Oh, Waa-nn-dah."

"That's enough," Mr. Meyers said.

There were more snickers from the back of the room.

"Settle down, class." Mr. Meyers turned toward me and quietly said, "If you want Leilani to tutor you, talk to me after school and I'll set it up," he said. "But if you would rather do it on your own, I can get materials together for you and your mom to work on at home." He turned his attention back to the class and said, "Okay, let's get back to work."

I walked down the aisle to my desk. My desk. My chair. Looking out my school window to the beautiful Koolau Mountains I missed so much.

"Page 183, Edgar Allan Poe." he said. "Rell, if you don't have your book with you, double up."

Double up—it was one of the first normal things anyone has told me to do in months.

A couple of times during class, I checked out kids I hadn't seen since September. Almost the whole school year had passed without me. The bulletin boards had notices up about prom bids and graduation tickets.

After English class, Jacqueline Maldonado gave me a present. In the hallway, some guy I didn't even know high-fived me and said he was glad I was back. Evelyn Dumas almost knocked me over with her hug, Sharlene Santos gave me a white ginger lei, and Nate Lee waved to me from the end of the hall.

It was easy to spot him. Six-foot-three, spiky black hair, and the world's greatest smile. But talking to him wouldn't be easy. The hall was jammed, and once I stepped out into the rush, I was swept away with the tide. Everybody was rushing, yelling, and bumping into each other. I cradled my backpack to my chest as tightly as I could.

Somehow, Nate and I got to each other.

"How's it?" he asked.

"Great. How's it with you?"

"Good."

Then nothing. *I already ran out of conversation with him.*

"There's a substitute teacher in math class," he said. "Yeah, Mrs. Marist had some kind of surgery."

We walked down the hall together.

"She's going to be out for the rest of the year," he said. "The sub is....well, you'll see." He stopped in front of Room 312. "This is my class....I've got to go."

"The new sub is what?"

Nate walked backwards into his class. "See you later."

"Later," I said.

My next class was history. Mr. Fujimoto welcomed me back; it took him a total of thirty seconds. It was short, polite, and to the point. No one gave me a lei, no one cheered, clapped or made a fuss about me being back. It was just what I had wished for.

Be careful of what you wish for.

History was a double period for me. Mr. Fujimoto lectured about the Civil War and Sherman's March to the Sea—certainly a relevant topic for fifteen-year-olds living in Hawaii who didn't know North from South. It was *mauka* or *makai,* that was enough.

By 10:30, I was getting drowsy. It was hard for me to sit still for so long. I hadn't sat at a desk in eight months, and I was used to getting up and walking around whenever I felt like it.

I lifted the tuberose lei and inhaled its sweetness. And I thought about Violet's Lei Shoppe on Maunakea Street. Violet's was a narrow stall. In front of the shop were refrigerator cases of strung lei, and in the back were lines of card tables piled with flower heads being strung by hunched-over old ladies who picked up the blossoms one by one and slid them down a long lei needle.

Somewhere, between daydreaming about Violet's, Mr. Fujimoto's lecture, and Dean Ujima's suck-up questions, it started to rain. Three cooing doves huddled under the eaves of the roof right outside the window.

I sketched the doves in my notebook. Then one flew away and there were two. Then the second one flew away.

When I was at Stanhope, I missed the sound of the doves cooing. I missed seeing the Koolau Mountains. I missed the mountains even more than the ocean—the clouds smoking around their peaks, the waterfalls, hiking the trails and smelling the mountain ferns.

"Am I making myself clear?" Mr. Fujimoto asked the class.

He was looking straight at me. I smiled, and nodded, and tried to look like I was paying attention. Then I checked the clock. I would have sworn it was going backwards. Then the bell. Then lunch.

Emi met me in the cafeteria. She offered to go through the food line for me, and I let her. I was tired—no, I was exhausted.

"Sure, a Diet Coke and a vegetarian chili," I said. "I'll get us a table."

When Emi got back, she put both trays on the table. "Sorry it took so long," she said. "The genius at the register couldn't make change for the soda machine."

Emi was wearing the star earring I bought for her in San Francisco. She sat down across from me and grinned. "It's great to have you back, Rell," she said.

"Thanks."

"And your makeup looks fab-u-lous," she said.

I lifted my chin. "I had it professionally done," I said.

"And look at you. That's my favorite," she said, reaching over to hold up the ginger lei. "So, how was it to be back?"

"You should have been in English class!" I said. "Kids stood up and clapped for me. They clapped like I was Miss America. Mr. Meyers was so nice, and kids gave me lei I should have got yesterday." I held up the wilted petals. "They were waiting for me to come back," I said.

"Told you," Emi said.

"And Jacqueline Maldonado gave me a present." I opened the small gold box and showed Emi the ceramic-angel pin inside.

"Oh, no. You're going to need that angel," Emi said. "Here comes Wanda Yamanaka headed straight for you."

"Re-ee-el." Only Wanda could turn my name into a three-syllable song.

"Welcome back, Rell." She kissed the top of my head.

I was sure she was testing to see if my hair was a wig or not.

"How are you, Rell?"

Do you really want to know, Wanda?

She brushed a few strands of hair from her face and followed it up with a wide-toothed smile. "Rell, you were so swamped after English class, we didn't get a chance to talk."

Wanda, we never talk.

"You are back at school, aren't you?" Her voice dripped with concern. "I mean for the rest of the year."

"Uh-huh."

"I've been so worried about you. I asked Emi about you every day. But you know how closed-mouthed she is." Wanda shot Emi a dirty look.

When I looked over at Emi, she was head-down in her pizza.

"Thanks."

Then without taking a breath, Wanda spewed a tragic story about her car getting scratched in the Neiman Marcus parking lot, and the rude security guard, and the uninterested store manager, and how her mother was canceling her Neiman's charge card because of the way she was treated.

"I'm sure Neiman's is crushed," Emi mumbled.

"You know, Rell." Wanda twisted her finger through her hair—her two-hundred-dollar-haircut hair, dyed-red Japanese hair. "I had a great idea for the school paper."

"All your ideas are great, Wanda." Emi rolled her eyes, but Wanda was oblivious.

"You could write an inspirational piece on what it was like to almost die." Wanda was almost cooing.

Emi dropped her pizza.

"I'd rather not," I said

"Then you could include a copy of it when you apply to colleges," Wanda said.

I thought not even Wanda could be this dense.

"I really don't think so," is what I said. It was a lot nicer than what I wanted to tell her to do with her idea.

"It could get you into a better college," Wanda said. "Your grades aren't the best," she added.

This was beyond belief. If it weren't for Sara Reynolds coming toward us, I might have cried.

"Welcome back, Sweetcakes." Sara gave me a big hug.

Wanda wedged herself between Sara and me. "Rell, I had another idea. The school paper could do a profile of you. You know, fighting cancer."

"Go for it, Rell," Emi said. "You can dress up like a sumo wrestler and fight a fat cancer cell. Throw in some Jell-O and the guys would all love it."

"What about playing it like Joan of Arc?" Sara said. "Now, there's a fighter."

Wanda was not amused. She eyeballed Sara from the top of her spiked hair to the tips of her blue-painted toenails. "Think about it, Rell. That kind of publicity could do you a lot of good."

I wanted to strangle Wanda with her own dyed-red hair.

Sara waved her hands in the air and pretended to sprinkle fairy dust over Wanda. "Be gone," she said.

"You are so weird." Wanda scowled.

Sara sprinkled her again.

"Weird," Wanda said. "Think about it, Rell." She walked away. "It's a great idea." Her words trailed behind her as she went away back to her own little galaxy where she was the only star.

"I owe you, Sara," I said.

Sara rippled her fingers in the air. "A sprinkle of gold dust and the troll is gone."

"I wouldn't waste the gold," Emi said.

"Silver doesn't penetrate collagen," Sara said.

"That's it!" I said. "I thought her lips looked bigger."

Sara put her index finger to her lips, mocking shooting an injection into them. "The better to gossip with, my dear."

I curled my lower lip down and thrust my tongue toward my nose.

"Good likeness," Emi said.

"Oh, Rell, I missed you so much." Sara hugged me again.

"The cards you sent to the hospital were the best," I said.

"Did you like the one of the hula dancer?"

"He was gorgeous," I said.

Sara bent her knees, tilted her pelvis, and rotated her hips. "Yes, he was."

"I taped him to my best friend's wall, hoping it would get her to visit Hawaii some day," I said, and as soon as I said it, I wanted to rewind that last remark and suck back my words. Why did I say "best friend?" Emi was my best friend. She also had an excellent sense of hearing and didn't let anything get by her.

I pictured my words flying across a computer screen into a file labeled "Emi will remember this forever, even if she never says anything to you." I looked over at her. She didn't register anything on her face. She had her eyes fixed on Sara.

"Anna." Sara waved Anna Cho over to the table, but she kept walking. Sara called her again.

Anna crept over to the table. I got up to give her a hug, but she moved back, not a full-step or even a half-step, nothing you could really notice, unless you felt it happening to yourself.

She was afraid of me, of cancer.

Kids at Stanhope talked about that all the time—that when they got home, some of their friends were afraid of "catching cancer." It was dumb, but so was Anna.

"Thanks for the balloon, Anna," I said, and decided I was going to hug her anyway, just to teach her a lesson—that she won't go home and die if she did.

Anna tensed up. "It was no big deal," she said.

I turned to Sara and Emi and said, "The balloons were in the shape of a rainbow." I wanted to see if Anna even knew what they looked like. "Did you pick them out?" I asked.

"Yeah," she said.

I never got any rainbow-shaped balloons.

Emi slid a chair toward Anna. "You want to sit with us?" she asked.

"I can't," Anna said. "I'm sitting with Makana, and you know how she get if she has to wait." She paused. "Maybe tomorrow?" she said.

"Sure," I said, knowing that tomorrow would never come.

Sara picked up her books. "I've got to go, too, Love Bug. I've got an Honor Society meeting. The new president is very anal about us being on time."

"Anal as in ass," Emi said.

"He wants to fix everything." Sara pumped up her biceps. "He's got real man issues."

I turned to Emi as if to ask who he was.

"Your oh-so-cute, Bondo-truck Nate Lee is the president," she said.

"A budding romance?" Sara raised her eyebrows.

"No!" I said. "Emi just's being a jerk."

After Sara left, Carol came by and gave me a lei, so did Karla and Kim and Trudy, and we pulled more chairs to our table and huddled around.

By the end of lunch I had been hugged, kissed and showered with so many lei of candy, ribbon, crocheted yarn, and plumeria that you really couldn't see my face—just like I imagined from Stanhope. But at Stanhope, there weren't Mylar balloons tied to my wrists or bouquets of drooping flowers. Almost everyone apologized to me, saying, "The flowers looked a lot better yesterday."

Kim Silva was the first person to ask me about my cancer. Sitting at the cafeteria table, in the middle of chomping down her Doritos and sipping her Diet Coke, she blurted out, "So what was cancer like?"

All conversation stopped. Everybody looked at Emi as if to ask her what to do next. It was funny. I knew they all wanted to ask the same question, but were afraid to ask. Only dear Kim, who honestly wanted to know what it was like, asked with the same curiosity she would ask about what it was like to have sex, or drive a truck, or have a tooth capped, broke the taboo.

I felt like I was the first one of us who got her period, and they all wanted to know the details. I acted like cancer was no big deal. I told them the funny stories I had practiced in the mirror that Sunday night. I told them stories about shopping for my wigs, and how I could fit into a size one dress now, instead of a seven.

"I'm so skinny that my collar bones hold up my bra." I tried to sound like a stand-up comedian.

Little by little, one nervous laugh after another, we all got more comfortable. Slowly, each girl told me about the rumors that were going around at school—that my leg got amputated, that I had a brain tumor, that I had six months to live, and my favorite—that I was dead. It was like a bad case of "telephone tag."

"Who said I was dying?" I asked.

"Wanda," Karla said. "Then I told Kim and she asked Emi if it was true."

Emi nodded. "It's true," she said.

"Well, if Wanda thought I was dying, why didn't she at least send me a card? You know, something from Neiman's card department?"

"We told you why," Emi said. "Because she was in the hospital herself—getting her lips done." Emi puckered up. "She did it just for you, Rell. She wanted to look good for your funeral."

The more they told me, the more I realized that it was Emi who stopped the rumor train from barreling me into the grave. Emi was my best friend.

After lunch, I wanted to thank her, but I let it wait. I wasn't going to gush all over her in the middle of the cafeteria. I was a spectacle as it was, the returning cancer girl loaded with flower lei and holding a billion Mylar balloons.

"You look tired," Emi said.

"You sound like my mother," I said, but in fact, I was exhausted. The lei were heavy and hot. My back hurt, and I had no energy to smile at one more person. But, I told myself, no matter what, I was going to keep going, and keep on smiling, because I wanted everyone to know that I was back, 100%, just like I was before.

But I knew I couldn't make it through one more class. I dropped my lei off in my locker, and I went to Mr. Owens to take him on his offer to get a Health Room pass. He was eating popcorn at his desk. Ugh! I could tell he was happy to give me the pass, and I was happy to get it.

I spent the rest of the day asleep. And when Mom picked me up after school, there were no questions. I piled the lei on the back seat, wedged in all the balloons, and said, "It was all fine, Mom, but I'm really tired." Then I pushed my seat back, closed my eyes, and slept the whole way home. I slept right up to dinnertime, when I figured I would be the center of attention, but I was wrong. It was Dad who had the big news that night.

CHAPTER FIVE

Somewhere between, "How was your first day back, Rell?" and "Pass the rice," Dad announced that his company bid on two new jobs: one was in Hilo, the other was in Guam. All I knew about Guam was that it was hot, humid, and the brown tree snakes killed all the birds there. I was scared to death we would have to move there, but Dad said if the company sent him to Guam, he would go by himself. I'm not sure Mom would have minded that.

Mom pushed her rice around the plate, and left most of her chicken untouched. She didn't ask Dad questions, she just listened, and stared at her plate like she was watching a Stephen King movie. She did drink, though. Three glasses of wine. And when Dad said he wouldn't mind it if he had to go to Guam by himself, she plunked her wine glass down on the table so hard, some of it splashed out.

"I'd get home about one weekend a month," Dad said.

I asked him what the chances were of getting the Hilo bid.

"Less than fifty-fifty," he said. They were the same odds I was giving their marriage.

For the rest of dinner, my head swiveled like a ping-pong ball. I talked to Mom; Mom talked to me. I talked to Dad; Dad talked to me. But neither of them talked to the other.

Right after dessert, I hightailed it to my room and got on the computer. I emailed LB about my first day at school. I told her about the lei, about English class, and about Wanda, but I didn't mention my parents fighting. I thanked her for all the photos of us, especially the ones of Tess. I missed Tess; I traced my finger over her face in the photo.

As soon as I got to bed, Ajax curled under the covers and snuggled against me, like a puppy against its mother. I wondered what it would be like to be a puppy in a big litter with all your brothers and sisters tossing and tumbling around you, playing all the time, and your parents not ever fighting.

I hated it when Mom and Dad fought. Before I got sick they fought like normal parents, but since then, they fought all the time.

On my second day back to school, I was feeling pretty good about being back. I thought the worst was over. Some kids asked questions, some kids stared, some kids shied away from me, but for the most part, it was a good. Yup, life was good, and then....

Enter Mrs. Cyril, the math sub from hell.

From the minute she took attendance, I knew I was in trouble.

"Estrella DeMello," she called.

"Here." I raised my hand.

She looked up and frowned. She looked like a cross between Ichabod Crane and every fairy tale wicked stepmother.

During the first ten minutes of class, we had a quiz. I wrote my name on the paper, and gave up after reading the first problem. While Mrs. Cyril corrected our quizzes, she assigned seatwork, just like in third grade. There was no way I could do those problems, either, so I put my head down and rested. It was a bad move; I fell asleep.

When I woke up, Mrs. Cyril was walking down the aisle, handing out our corrected quiz sheets. She read each student's name, then stood over them, holding their paper in front of them before she let it go. She smiled at some students, and told them they did a good job. I wasn't one of them.

When she stood next to me, she said, "The average grade on this quiz was 68%. The median was 75. Had it not been for some incredibly low scores, the mean could have been two percentage points higher. Those of you who failed this quiz, don't have the slightest idea of what I said." She handed me my paper. "Mean, median, average. It may as well be Greek to you."

I scored a whopping zero.

"Clearly, some of you should not be in this class." She spit when she spoke. "Until the class average is 80, we will continue to have quizzes on this chapter."

Everybody groaned.

Mrs. Cyril said in a voice loud enough for everybody to hear, "Estrella, perhaps you should consider getting a tutor." She stared at me.

Screw you, I thought. I've stared down a lot worse than you. I beat cancer. Didn't anybody tell you?

For the rest of the class, I didn't hear a word she said. I fantasized about her going to the principal to complain about me, and then the principal telling her I had cancer. He would make her apologize to me in front of the whole class, and then he would fire her, right there on the spot.

I was still ranting about Cyril to Emi after school. My mom let Emi drive me home. It was one more step back to being normal.

When I got into Emi's car, I slammed the door. "She is such a dried-up bitch," I said. "Who does she think she is? She's a lousy sub."

"Want to stop by Coconut Joe's and get a drink?" Emi asked.

"Sure," I said.

Emi put on her seatbelt and started the car.

"The woman can't get a *real* teaching job," I said.

"I heard that the first ten times you said it," Emi said.

"It's true." I reached over and changed the radio station to oldies.

"I was listening to that station," Emi said.

"I'm sick of Hawaiian music," I said.

"Hmm, anything else bothering you?" Emi looked over at me. "Does the princess want the air-conditioning cooler? The seat adjusted? How about a pillow for her royal ass?"

"She's a lousy sub," I said. "A shitty-low life."

Emi pulled in to the Coconut Joe's parking lot and pointed at some college guys sitting outside. "Check them out," she said.

There was a table of older guys in Pacific University T-shirts huddled around a table crammed with laptops, notebooks, and cigarettes.

Emi walked directly in front of their table. She walked slower than usual. She didn't look at them but laughed about Cyril in a fake drama-class kind of way.

"I wish I could transfer to a different high school," I said.

She turned to me and said, "Let's not advertise the fact that we're in high school, okay?"

"Who cares?" I said.

"I care," she said, and then she pasted a phony smile on her face, and glanced over at the guys.

She looked ridiculous.

"Grab the table next to them," she said.

"They're smoking," I said.

"Just do it." She flipped her hair off her shoulders and smiled.

"No." There was no way. Hodgkin's Disease + radiation to the chest + smoking = lung cancer.

I followed Emi inside and ordered my own drink. When we got outside, she headed straight for the table next to the guys.

"The table is upwind of them," Emi said. "You won't breathe in any smoke."

She didn't give me a chance to fight. She sat down, and dragged her chair so that it faced directly at them.

I was still fuming about Cyril.

"Relax," Emi said. "The guys are looking at us."

"What a bitch! She's a lousy sub!"

"Everyone here already knows that, Rell." Emi smiled at the guys, and shrugged her shoulders.

"I bet she's been a sub her whole life. Life? She probably doesn't have a life."

Emi leaned over, and dug her fingers into my forearm. "Rell, if you don't stop it, they're going to get up and leave."

"Does she care that I've been poisoned, radiated, and cut wide open?"

"No so loud, Rell."

"I almost died!"

"You didn't almost die," Emi said.

"Well, I almost almost died."

"No points for almost almost, Rell."

"I'm bald. Do I get points for that?"

"You're scaring them away." Emi never let go of her smile.

And I did scare them away. They got up, closed up their laptops, and moved around the corner of the building.

Who cares?

"See what you've done?" Emi said.

One of them shook his head as he walked away.

"Emi, they're college guys. Don't you think they know we're fifteen-year old virgins who wouldn't know what to do?"

"Well, they do now, Miss Virgin-Forever-I-Almost-Died." Emi clutched her throat. "I was cut open, tortured, and I'm bald. Pity me, please."

"Okay," I said. "I'm sorry. But...."

"Too late," Emi said.

"What if I dance naked on the table? Do you think that would get them back here?"

"Only if you twirled your wig in the air while you danced," Emi said.

"Deal," I said and we linked our pinky fingers.

"You know what, Rell." Emi grinned. "You should take your wig off in math class. Picture it. You spin it around your finger, and hurl it at Cyril. She screams. She falls to the floor gasping for breath. You're the only one in class who knows CPR. She begs you to help her, but you refuse. And with her last dying breath she screams, 'Forgive me, Estrella.'"

"She's a bitch."

"Lighten up, Rell."

I mocked a stupid smile and said, "This is me lightened up."

"Come on, Rell. Even cancer patients are allowed to laugh."

She had no right to say what cancer patients were allowed to do.

Emi pulled her chair closer to me. "Don't get mad at me, Rell, but maybe Cyril is right. Maybe you could use a tutor. If you got a tutor it would get her off your back and you could catch up faster."

"I don't need a tutor."

"Rell, you've never been a math genius."

"I don't need a tutor."

"You're going to flunk math and end up taking it in summer school."

I knew she was right.

"Sara could tutor you," Emi said.

"She's too busy."

"Maybe she could match you up with someone from the Honor Society," Emi said.

"Right, some social zero with a computer he calls Honey Girl."

"You never know," Emi said. "Maybe he'll turn out to be a gorgeous hula dancer with incredible thighs."

There it was. She heard me make the remark about the hula dancer's thighs. That meant she heard me call LB my "best friend."

I felt like a sleazy soap opera husband who was in love with two different women. And in a weird way, I understood that guy, because I had two best friends. There was Emi, my best friend for life, and there was LB at Stanhope, fighting for her life.

The next day at school, Nate Lee stopped at our lunch table. "Hey, Rell, do you have a minute?" he said.

"Rell and I are having lunch alone," Emi said without giving me much of a chance to answer him.

"It's about your math class," he said.

I handed my soda cup to Emi. "Would you mind filling this for me?" I gritted my teeth and plastered a smile on my face. "Please." I bulged out my eyes as if it say, "Do not blow this for me!"

She grabbed the cup, but she didn't budge.

Nate put his foot up on the chair next to me, and rested his cafeteria tray on his knee. He was wearing a Year of the Dragon T-shirt.

I looked over at Emi. "My soda?"

"Anything for you, Princess." She bowed and walked away.

Nate looked down at his tray. When Emi was gone, he said, "Rell, I'm not bragging, but…."

I had no idea what he was going to say.

"I have a 97 average in math," he said.

"Is that a 97 average, or a 97 mean, or median?" I said.

"Average." He smiled.

"So, if you want help." He paused. "I mean, if you want a tutor…." His voice trailed off.

"So you heard I'm the class dummy?" I said.

"I heard Cyril was a jerk to you." He smiled again, and I imagined what he looked like in second grade. He probably had the same smile.

"I'm a good tutor, Rell."

Here I was, in the middle of the school cafeteria and Nate Lee, a junior, was asking me out. Well, maybe not asking me out, but asking to tutor me.

"I wouldn't charge you anything," he said.

Be cool, I thought. Just breathe.

"Let me ask my parents," I said. My heart was beating so loud I could hear it.

"I know how it is to miss a lot of school," he said.

I nodded. "Emi told me you were out a lot because your grandfather died."

He looked puzzled. "My grandfather died when I was three," he said.

"Still here, Nate?" Emi was back with a filled soda cup.

"It looks like it," he said.

"Well, you can leave now. Emi and I are having lunch—alone."

Nate looked at me and smiled. "Think about it," he said.

I smiled back. "Hey," I said pointing to his shirt. "Were you born in the Year of the Dragon?" The dragon on his shirt was deep green with flaming breath that curled into daggers of smoke.

"No. Year of the Tiger," he said. "Tigers are fearless, gallant, and smart," he said, and left.

"Fearless, gallant, and smart," Emi mocked Nate. "He forgot conceited, arrogant, and pushy."

"You're not being fair, Emi."

Emi cocked her head and fluttered her eyelashes. "Were you born in the Year of the Dragon?"

"What is it with you and him? Do you two have a history I don't know about?"

"Me and Tiger Boy? I don't think so."

"Well, what then?"

"I don't know. I don't trust him."

"All he did was offer to tutor me in math," I said.

"You don't know anything about him," Emi said.

"Right. He's a serial killer masquerading as an honor society president."

"He's a social zero. There's no masquerading that."

"I'm going to say yes."

"What about Sara?"

"What about her?"

"I give up," Emi said. "But don't come running to me when you find out Tiger Boy is an idiot."

During the rest of the afternoon, I fantasized about what it would be like to have Nate as a tutor. I pictured the two of us studying in the library. Everybody would stare at us. We would lean into each other over our books. Nate would ask if he could take me home. We'd be at my house. Alone.

I couldn't stop thinking about him. I pictured him riding a surfboard, him wearing red hibiscus print board shorts. I imagined him playing basketball in a torn University of Hawaii T-shirt. I saw him running the beach. He would stop when he saw me sitting under a palm tree. Ajax would run over to him. He would pet the dog, and Ajax would jump him. By the end of the day, I had our first three kids named.

I caught up to him in the parking lot.

"I talked to my mom," I said. So what if it was a lie. "And she thinks it's a good idea for you to tutor me."

"Okay," Nate said. "It's a deal. Let's do it."

"Okay," I said.

"When do you want to start?" he asked. "Four-thirty at Starbucks?"

"You mean today?"

"If we're going to do this thing, yeah."

"Wow! You do work fast," I said. "But I can't today. I've got an appointment. What about tomorrow?"

"Tomorrow," he said, "right after school. I'll pick you up on the soccer field side of the parking lot."

"I'll be there," I said.

"Great."

"Great," I repeated.

When I got home from school that day, Mom was waiting for me in the kitchen. "Dr. Maitlin called," she said. "She's running about fifteen minutes late. So on the way over I'm going to stop at the dry cleaners."

That was fine with me. I was still thinking about Nate. We were at the prom, dancing a slow dance. I was wearing a teal satin dress. No, change that to a skinny little black dress with high black heels and shimmering stockings. Nate would give me a nine-strand *pikake* lei and I'd give him a *maile* lei.

I wondered if I should tell Dr. Maitling about Nate, even though I knew it was crazy. Here was this guy who talked to me a total of five times in my life, and one time was in a parking lot when he shouted "Hi" from his truck.

He asked to be your tutor you, Rell, not to marry you and have his babies.

There really wasn't much to tell. Besides, I didn't want to jinx anything before it happened.

I imagined my first tutoring session with Nate. I wondered if I should act dumb at first, then learn really fast, so he could think he's a great tutor. I wondered if I should smile a lot, or look serious, look into his eyes, or look down. Perfume or not? Jeans or dress?

Get a grip, Rell.

By time we arrived at Dr. Maitlin's, I decided to wear my red hoop earrings and my lemongrass cologne. It wasn't too sweet, and it had the right amount of tang.

Mom left me at the front door of the clinic. The routine was that she would go to the health food store while I was in my session, and an hour later, she'd pick me up in the same spot in the parking lot.

"I love you, Rell," she said. The more nervous Mom got, the more times she told me she loved me. "Do you want anything at the store?" she asked.

"Nope."

"I love you, Honey."

"I love you, too, Mom."

I walked into the clinic and got in the elevator. I checked myself out in the mirror on the ceiling. I did look good upside down! Then I walked down the hall of Dr. Maitlin's floor, past the doors of offices of specialists.

There was Dr. Hirota, a cardiologist, like the cardiologist who shoved pipe-sized tubes in my veins to check my heart for damage from chemotherapy. And the pulmonary specialists, like the guys who measured the diminished capacity of my lungs—from my chemotherapy. The gynecologist, like Dr. Sato, who held my hand when he told me I may or may not be able to have children, and there was no way to test for it either. Once more, a bonus of chemotherapy. But Dr. Sato was kind when he explained stuff to me.

Since I started treatment, my periods stopped. And they still hadn't started. I knew it was normal for it to come back slow after treatment, but I was afraid that it meant I'd never be able to have a baby. If Dr. Sato lived in Hawaii, I could ask him.

I kept walking down the hall, past the pediatric oncology group—the guys who treated kids with cancer. Just catching a glimpse of a bald-headed kid, or a kid with a bloated face made me want to run away. I didn't want to be part of them. Dr. Maitlin told me that kind of thinking was normal.

Dr. Maitlin was about fifty years old, blond, athletic, and funny. She drove yellow Saab convertible to work on weekdays, and on weekends, she drove a beat-up pickup truck to the stables where she rode horses. She always sat up straight. Her blouses were starched, and she smelled of expensive perfume. My appointments with her started out the same. At first, we would talk about nothing. She would ask me how things were going and I would say, "Fine." It would go on like that until she figured out what I really wanted to talk about.

"You went back to school this week," Dr. Maitlin said.

"Yup."

"How was that?" she asked.

"Not bad." I looked over at her collection of plastic dinosaurs, monsters, and dragons.

"Did anybody say anything that made you feel uncomfortable?"

"No. It wasn't like that," I said. "Some kids got nervous around me, just like you said they might."

"And?"

"English class was cool," I told her. "It was my first class. The teacher made a big deal over me. Kids gave me lei, and they stood up, and clapped for me."

"How did that make you feel?" she asked."

"Like I deserved it," I said.

"Deserved it how?" Dr. Maitlin crossed her legs. She kept an open notebook on her lap.

"It was like what I thought would happen when I left Stanhope.

I thought all the doctors and nurses would line up along the hall and clap and hug me when I walked out—like it was a graduation."

"What did happen at Stanhope?"

"The nurses came in my room to say goodbye, and I went to see Nick. I told you about him, right?"

"Yes," she said. "And Nick died the next week."

"Two weeks later," I said.

"What else happened?"

"Right before I left, Dr. Braden came in. He talked to Mom and me about follow-ups with the doctors here. Then he hugged me and that was it."

I looked over at the clock. I had twenty minutes left in the session.

Dr. Maitlin pointed the toe of her crossed leg toward the ceiling. Whenever she did that, I knew that she was going to ask me a tough question. "Your mother called me on Monday night," she said.

"I know." I rolled my eyes.

"She was upset about you cutting school."

"She's always upset."

"She's worried about you, Rell."

I threw my head back on the chair. "All my mother does is worry. She asks me a million questions a day. How are you, Sweetheart? Are you hungry, Sweetheart? Are you tired, Honey? Last week she even wanted to feel my neck where the cancer used to be." I felt the tears building in my eyes. I yanked a tissue out of the box.

"She's always doing stuff like that," I said. "Once I caught her watching me sleep. I was in bed, I woke up, and I saw her standing at the door. She was watching me sleep!"

Dr. Maitlin pushed her eyeglasses back up her nose.

"She makes me feel like some kind of cancer bomb that's ready to blow."

Dr. Maitlin took folded up papers out of her notebook and handed them to me. "Your mother sent me a schedule of your follow-up tests."

"This is my personal stuff!"

"She wanted me to be aware of those times when you may feel stressed."

"She had no right to give you these."

"It's her way to take care of you, Rell."

I flipped the pages reading Mom's notes in the margins. "I have every one of these dates on my wall calendar, and she knows it."

"Sometimes it's hard for parents to stop fighting cancer," Dr. Maitlin said. "They can't let go of it."

"Then tell her to get her own cancer." As soon as I said it, I was sorry I did. I wouldn't wish cancer on anybody. "I didn't mean that," I said. "But she treats me like such a baby."

"Your mother sees you as her baby."

"I'm fifteen," I said. "Girls my age are having babies, and I still have to ask permission to go to the mall. All my mother thinks about when it comes to me is cancer. I don't exist anymore. Every time she looks at me, I know she's thinking: It's going to come back. My baby has cancer. Just look at her.'" I wiped my cheek with my hand. "I hate it."

"If you had a choice, what would you want her to do?" Dr. Maitlin asked.

"I don't know," I said. "I guess I'd want her to forget I ever had cancer."

"Can you?"

"That's not a fair question," I said.

"Why not?"

"It's unfair."

"By whose rules?"

I leaned back in the chair, tearing my tissue into shreds. I wasn't going to answer that question and I was going to sit there for the rest of the session and not talk. It worked for a while.

"How's your friend Emi?" Dr. Maitlin asked.

"Okay."

"Did you do anything together lately?"

"Not really," I answered.

"How about homework? Are you handling it?"

"Uh-huh."

"And your dog? Is he okay?"

I nodded.

She was fishing for something to get me talking again, but I wasn't falling for her tricks. At the end of my session, I stood up, shoved my tissues in my backpack, and walked to the door. My hand was on the doorknob when I turned around and said, "I think my parents are going to get a divorce." I watched to see what kind of reaction I would get from Dr. Maitlin. There was none.

"They fight all the time, and it's always about me."

She took off her glasses. "We'll talk about this next time, Rell—at the beginning of the session."

CHAPTER SIX

By my second week back at school, most kids didn't notice me anymore. I was beginning to feel normal, although there were a few kids who reminded me that I wasn't.

There were the "well-wishers" who told me about every cancer survivor doing every great thing there was to do. They told me about survivors who played National League Hockey, owned billion-dollar Internet companies, who were Senators, Congressmen, and TV actors. They wore LIVESTRONG bracelets and smiled at me like I was their favorite cause.

I didn't want hear stories about what great things survivors did. I wanted to meet that one survivor who could look me in the eye and say, "I'm cured," without crossing her fingers or holding her breath. The one survivor who wasn't afraid of cancer in the middle of the night.

Some kids at school called me heroic or brave. I wasn't heroic. Heroes have choices. I wasn't brave either. When the chemotherapy nurse walked in my room, I cried before she even touched me. And when my treatment was over, and I went back to my room, and I cried some more.

The chemotherapy drugs didn't care if I was brave or if I cried. Either they worked or they didn't. They didn't care—just like cancer.

When Dr. Braden said, "You have cancer," I cried. The problem was, when my treatment was over he didn't say, "You don't have cancer anymore." He said, "We find no evidence of cancer."

"No evidence"—like a weed in a garden, creeping under the ground, until one day, a pale green shot pops through the ground, and chokes the blossoming flowers.

I hated cancer.

At school, a girl I didn't even know came up to me and told me she read a book called *The Summer of My Tears*. She said it was about a blonde cheerleader who got cancer in April, almost died in June, was cured in August, and in November she was crowned Homecoming Queen. It sounded just like my life, except for the part about being blond, a cheerleader, Homecoming Queen, and cured.

I wanted to ask if the book described how your hair falls out in clumps on your pillow, or how your mouth oozes with sores after radiation. But I could tell she wanted only polite answers. Nothing too scary or too close.

There were times I got angry and incredibly mean. Once, in Spanish class, I made a list of all the people I knew who should have got cancer instead of me, but I quickly crumpled it up.

Kids would ask me, "How could you tell you had cancer?" I wanted to tell them that one morning I was taking a shower, and I felt a small boob growing out of my neck, and when the surgeons cut it out, they found it full of cancer.

A few kids would say things to me like, "I read on the Internet that Hodgkin's disease is rare."

"Yup," I would say. "But it doesn't matter if you're the one who got it."

What they wanted it to do was line my life against theirs and convince themselves that cancer could never happen to them. It could only happen to somebody else. I couldn't blame them; I did the same thing myself when I was in treatment.

Whenever somebody died at Stanhope, I would convince myself that it could never happen to me. My cancer was different from theirs, they never did well in treatment, my doctors were better than theirs were.

I held on to my belief that I would be cured, and that when I was finished with treatment, I would go back to being me again. Just Rell, not the girl with cancer. But it didn't work. I couldn't forget it, ignore it, or pretend it didn't exist.

I divided my life into two parts: My life before cancer, and my life after. There were so many "before" things that went along with cancer—like before Tess's funeral, before Mom and Dad fought all the time, before the nightmares.

The nightmares first started when I was in chemo. Some kids got them, some didn't—I was one of the unlucky ones. I had horrible nightmares. At first they came only during the week of and the week after chemo. Then they started to come anytime.

The week after Tess died, I had a nightmare about fairies, thieves, and a red-haired girl who thought she had a beautiful voice. She sang to the birds and the clouds, and, at night, she stood at the edge of the beach and asked the wind to carry her song. But when she opened her mouth to sing, her voice was sharp and off-key, and shiny black eels flowed out of her mouth.

The first time I had that dream, I woke up screaming. LB called the night nurse. The nurse held me, and rocked me. She wiped my face with a cool towel. She changed my sheets, took my vital signs, and then made a note in my medical file.

After the nurse left, LB pulled a chair next to my bed. She bundled herself up in an afghan, put her head on my bed, and slept there for the rest of the night.

But kids at school didn't want to hear stories like that. They wanted a fairy tale like, "Once upon a time, Estrella DeMello got cancer, then she got better and lived happily ever after," like a long-haired princess rescued by a charming prince.

The closest thing to a prince I had in my life was Nate Lee, who didn't ride into my life on a white stallion. He drove up in a beat-up, Bondo-ed pick up truck with split green vinyl seats and a rusted out floor.

Nate was under-romantic and over-logical. But he was my prince; he was a cheap prince. He took me to half-priced movies, free nights at the Waikiki Zoo, and "Girls Play Free" night at the Waikiki Bowl-O-Rama.

Nate had a great smile and beautiful hands. I noticed Nate's hands the first time he tutored me. When he talked, he waved them through the air like an orchestra conductor, and he would chop the air sharply when he emphasized a point.

He was explaining how to calculate a median when I asked him, "Do you play the piano?"

"Why?" he asked. "Is there a way to explain calculating a median using piano keys?"

"I don't know." I laughed. "I was looking at your fingers. They're so long and graceful. Perfect for playing the piano."

"You and my grandmother!" He formed an X with his hands and backed away from me.

"Is she that bad?" I asked.

"My San Francisco grandmother was determined to make me a musical prodigy. She's straight out of *The Joy Luck Club.* 'Na-than, you be good piano play-ah.' Once she bribed a fortune-teller to tell my parents that music was my destiny."

"Did you ever take lessons?" I asked.

"Did I have a choice? My grandmother paid for a year of piano lessons. Then she came to Hawaii for my recital. After she heard me play, she gave up."

"Were you that bad?"

"Not only was I bad, but I was an ungrateful grandchild, and all of China was ashamed of me."

"Hmm. Sounds serious."

"She's still disappointed."

"I know how that goes," I said. "My father wants me to be an engineer."

"What do you want to be?" he asked.

I just want to be alive.

After a few weeks together, Wanda Yamanaka declared Nate and me boyfriend and girlfriend. It would have all been true except for one minor detail. Nate still hadn't kissed me.

At the end of each email from LB, she would ask, "Did he kiss you yet?" My answer was always the same, "I'm working on it." The problem was that Nate wasn't.

One night, LB finally asked, *Do you think he's gay?* It was something I was wondering myself.

I don't think so, I wrote back to her. Maybe he is only a nice guy, and a good tutor.

Then one night, five weeks and three days after our first tutoring session, on a moonlit Friday night, Nate kissed me!

I emailed LB as soon as I got home.

I wrote to her that after the movies, we went to the beach to look at the moon. I was standing there, looking up, and Nate walked up behind me. He put his arms around me, and he kissed my neck. He k-i-s-s-e-d my neck.

LB instantly messaged me back. *Give me all the details,* she wrote.

What are you doing up? I wrote. It was one a.m. in San Francisco.

I'm planning our Grand Canyon trip, she answered. *But forget about the Grand Canyon, tell me all about tonight.*

It was great, I wrote.

"Rell." Mom knocked on the door. I closed my computer screen.

"Did you and Nate have a good time tonight?" she asked.

"Uh-huh."

"Dad and I thought you would be home sooner," she said.

"I was home before ten, Mom."

"But you need your sleep, Sweetheart."

"Okay," I said. I wasn't going to argue, I'd lose anyway, and I'd be wasting time I could be emailing LB. "Sorry," I said. "Nate and I were talking, and I guess I should have come home sooner." I sounded like the perfect daughter.

Mom walked over to my desk and kissed the top of my head. "Are you doing homework?" She gestured toward my computer.

"No." I shook my head. "I'm emailing LB."

"Tell her I send my love." Mom paused, then she said, "Emi called. She wants to go shopping with you tomorrow. You know, Sweetheart, Emi may be feeling a little left out these days. You've been spending a lot of time with Nate."

"He's my tutor."

"And the rest of the time you're together? What do you call that?"

I knew she was right.

"Emi said the Sassafras store is going out of business."

"I hate shopping," I said.

"Rell, when was the last time you went out with her?"

"I don't know." *Why did she have to ruin the night of my first kiss with Nate?*

"I think you owe it to Emi to go with her."

"Fine. What time does she want to go?"

"She said she'll call you in the morning, but, Rell." Another pause.

Great. What did she want now?

Mom lowered her voice, and tone got serious. "Before you go with Emi, Dad and I want to with you."

My cancer must be back.

"Did Dr. Braden call?" *Something must have shown up on one of my tests.*

"No," Mom said. "Nothing like that."

They were getting divorced.

"So, what's it about?" I asked.

"Nothing important. It can wait until morning."

I wanted to ask her if it was so important, what was all the drama about? But I let it go. I had more important things on my mind. I wanted to get back to LB and tell her about my first kiss with Nate.

As soon as my mother left, I flipped up my computer, and wrote to LB, *Something's up with my parents.*

Focus, Rell, she wrote. *It's about the kissing.*

Kiss, I corrected her. *Not kissing.*

I told LB that all night I knew that Nate wanted to kiss me, or I was hoping he did. I caught him staring at me at the movies, and then afterwards, when we went to Tropical Freeze for an ice cream, he watched me eat. That's when he asked me if I wanted to go to the beach on the way home, I was sure he wanted to kiss.

And then what? LB wrote.

We were walking on the beach, kind of close together, but not touching. Nate had his hands in his pockets. Then he put his arm around me, and we both froze, like we were both waiting for me to say something, or for him to do something, but neither of us did. We walked a little more, and then we stopped, I stood there and looked up at the moon. That's when he kissed my neck.

More, LB wrote.

There isn't any more.

Is he a good kisser? She asked.

I'll ask my neck.

Was it an open mouth or closed? She asked.

My neck said it was open.

Oh my God! LB wrote. *I can feel his lips on me right now.*

LB wanted details.

There are no details, I wrote to her. *Nothing. Nada. Zip.*

Once she was convinced it was one neck kiss, and that I couldn't see it happen, she switched to talking about our Grand Canyon trip.

I rub my fire agate stone every night before I go to sleep, LB wrote.

LB's fire agate stone was a copper-colored stone that was flecked with streaks of gold. Her parents bought it for her when they took her brother to the Grand Canyon. LB was supposed to go with them. All the plans were made, and then she got an infection, and had to stay in the hospital.

I found a three-day llama trek that takes you to the bottom of the canyon, she wrote. *It costs two thousand dollars and you sleep in tents.*

Llamas spit, I wrote. *Besides, that's about fifteen hundred dollars more than I have.*

LB told me that the tour company was looking for junior photographers to take actions shots during the trip. Then the company sells the photos to the tourists to make extra money.

It sounds like a spoof on the Travel Channel, I wrote.

Rell, will you think about it?

I don't know how to take pictures that are good enough to sell, I wrote.

They teach you.

I'll think about, I wrote, but I knew there was no way I was going to travel with llamas and sleep in a tent.

Good, she wrote. *Because I've already sent for two applications. Yours is going to your house.*

My mom will love that, I wrote.

How is your mom? LB wrote.

Awful, I wrote. *If she could hire someone to follow me around to take my vital signs all day, she would. I'd probably have blood drawn every three hours.*

Speaking of blood, LB wrote, *the vampire techs send their love. They paid me a visit about an hour ago.*

Why are you getting your blood tested at night? I asked LB. I knew that late night visits to draw blood weren't routine.

My counts have been low, and Doc Lynch is being careful.

Are you still getting treatment? I asked.

Yes, LB wrote.

Blood counts ruled the life of chemo patients. If your counts were too high, or too low, your treatment might be postponed, or cancelled. And, as much as I hated getting chemo, I panicked whenever one of my sessions was cancelled.

Is Dr. Lynch worried about you?

He didn't say anything to me, she answered.

Are your parents there?

Another sure giveaway that the doctors were worried about you was that they'd have all your parents come in for a consultation.

No, my mom's at home, LB wrote. *My brother's got the flu and my mom is afraid that she could pass it to me. Besides, my dad's been working an extra-shift to pay for my bills, so at least my brother has my mom to himself for a while.*

Have you had any nosebleeds? I wrote.

No.

Fever?

No.

Rashes.

No. No night sweats, no sudden loss of weight. Stop it, Rell. You sound like a zit-faced intern.

Stanhope was a teaching hospital. That meant that every few weeks a new batch of interns rotated through the cancer ward, and asked us the same questions that every other batch of newbies asked.

Sorry, I wrote.

It's okay, she wrote. *I was wondering why they were doing the blood tests myself.*

But you're feeling fine? I needed to be reassured.

Yeah, she wrote. *But I'm tired. I've been up since six and it's almost 2 a.m.*

Go to bed, LB, I wrote.

Yeah, and I'll be dreaming about Nate, she answered.

I love you, LB, I wrote.

Right back at you, Rell.

The next morning I woke up to the smell of one of Dad's Saturday morning breakfasts: pancakes, bacon, scrambled eggs, and freshly squeezed orange juice.

Dad was pouring Mom a cup of coffee when I walked in the kitchen. She put down her newspaper and thanked him for the coffee. She was as polite to him as she would be to a coffee-shop waiter.

"Morning, Mom."

"Morning, Sweetheart," she said. "Emi called about an hour ago. She'll be here in twenty minutes," Mom said.

I checked the clock. It was nine o'clock.

"She said she wanted to be there when the doors open at ten," Mom said.

"Why didn't you wake me up?" I squatted down to pet Ajax. "Good boy," I said. I let him lick my face.

"Rell, I told you not to—"

"Let the dog lick your face." I finished her sentence for her in a mock singsong voice. "You could get rabies or worse yet, you could get doggie cancer."

"That's not funny, Rell," Mom said.

"It is funny, Mom."

"Dogs carry disease," she said.

I poured myself a glass of orange juice. "It's okay, Mom, I just read about a new vaccine for doggie cancer. I'm safe now," I said.

"How is my Estrella this morning?" Dad lifted his pancake spatula high over my head and gave me a hug.

"Just wonderful, Dad."

"What can I get you? Two pancakes or three?"

"One pancake," I said

"Bacon or sausage?"

"Bacon."

"Bagel or toast?"

"Bagel."

As Dad and I went through our Saturday morning ordering ritual, I watched my mother out of the corner of my eye. She was glaring at Dad.

"David, talk to her," Mom said.

"What would you like me to talk to her about, Maria? The pressure per square inch of the concrete we're pouring on the job site?"

"It's not on my need-to-know list, Dad," I said.

"Damnit, David. This is what I was talking about. You get to be the good guy, and I'm always the monster."

"Let's not start off the day like this, Maria," Dad said.

"No," Mom said. "Let's pretend everything is just wonderful."

"It is wonderful, Mom." Why couldn't she see that?

"Tell her, David," Mom said.

Dad put down the spatula. "Your mother read about a veter-inarian who quit taking care of dogs because he was diagnosed with Hodgkin's disease."

"So?" I said.

"Your mother read that—"

"Stop right there, David," Mom said. "It isn't that I read this or I read that. It's a medical fact."

"Okay," Dad said. "It a medical fact that having a dog may be a serious health risk for you." He sounded apologetic.

"You must be kidding." I turned to Mom.

"Rell, you have to be aware of the risks of your condition," Mom said.

"I cannot believe this." I looked at Dad for some support.

"Hear your mother out on this one, Rell," he said.

I threw up my hands in the air. "Now Ajax is a health threat. Maybe I should tattoo a Surgeon's General Warning on his neck."

"Dogs carry a virus that can kill you," Mom said.

"Bacon can kill me. Eggs can kill me."

"Rell, you don't know what having a dog in the house could do to you. You let him sleep with you, he licks your face. You don't know the risk you're taking," Mom said.

"And what do you think your second-hand smoke does to me?"

Dad snapped. "Do not speak to your mother like that, young lady."

Dad just switched sides.

"I was talking about the dog," I said. "At night, Ajax sneaks cig-arettes in the garage like nobody's supposed to know he's doing it."

"That's enough!" Dad pointed his finger at my face. "You apol-ogize to your mother, right now."

"I'm sorry." I cocked my head, and stared out the window.

"That was a half-assed apology if I ever heard one," Dad said. "Try again."

"I'm sorry." I said it with enough remorse to keep myself out of trouble.

"The article said that some dogs carry a virus that could be fatal to cancer patients, particularly to Hodgkin's patient," Mom said.

"Can I call Dr. Braden and ask him what he thinks?" I said.

"I already did," she said.

"What did he say?"

"I left a message for him," Mom said. "Certainly, you know that we won't do anything about Ajax until we hear from him."

"What exactly does 'do anything about Ajax' mean?" I was screaming. "Are you getting rid of him?"

"No, Sweetheart—"

"Do *not* call me Sweetheart while you're talking about taking my dog away."

"We're not going to take him away," Mom said.

I looked at Dad. "Well, what are you talking about?"

"We don't know yet," Dad said.

"I'm not the boy in the space suit! I had cancer," I yelled it loud enough for the whole neighborhood to hear.

"Rell." Dad put his hand on my shoulder.

"Leave me alone." I jerked away from him.

"We want only the best for you," Dad said.

Only the best for your little Estrella.

"You can't protect me from everything, Dad."

"Rell," Mom said. "What if Dr. Braden says that it's dangerous for you to have Ajax in the house?"

"That's crazy, Mom. I talked about Ajax all the time. He saw pictures of him on my wall. Don't you think he would have said something?" Ajax circled my feet. "Do you think I'm the first Hodgkin's patient in the history of the world to have a dog?" I picked up Ajax, held him close to me, and let him lick my face. "See. There. I let him lick me and I'm still alive!"

"Can you please put the dog down?" Mom said.

"No."

"Please, Rell."

No. Not this time. I'm not giving in.

"This is getting blown out of proportion," Mom said.

"I don't know. Getting rid of Ajax is a big proportion to me." I could not believe that in five minutes, the morning went from pancakes and bacon, to taking away Ajax. "If I go out with Emi, will Ajax be here when I get back?" I asked.

"Of course, he will," Dad said.

"Mom?"

"The dog will be here, Rell," Mom said. "We're not some kind of monsters," she said. "We're just concerned."

Be less concerned.

CHAPTER SEVEN

I stomped down to my room and took a shower. I turned the water on full blast, stood under it, and cried. *When exactly did my parents lose their minds?*

I replayed all the conversations Dr. Braden and I had about Ajax at the hospital. I remembered him asking how long we had had him and what kind of dog he was.

I told him he was a *poi* dog, a twenty-five-pound, mixed-breed mutt.

He thought I said a coy dog, and that he didn't know they had coy dogs in Hawaii.

Dr. Braden knew I had a dog. He knew it. I convinced myself that Dr. Braden would have said something to me if I couldn't keep Ajax. I was sure of it—I wasn't crazy. My mom was crazy, and my dad was too afraid of her to back me up.

Forget them. I'll just go out with Emi, I thought. I figured that by the time I got back home, everything would be worked out. *But what if it wasn't? What if they were going to get rid of Ajax?*

I got dressed, put on my makeup, and marched myself through the kitchen and right out the front door without saying goodbye to either one of them. Then I paced up and down in the driveway until Emi pulled up.

I got in her car, and tossed a copy of *Celebrity Secrets* off the front seat on to the floor. "They have lost their minds!" I said as I pulled my seat belt out, but it jammed halfway across my chest. "Stupid thing." I pulled it out again.

"I assume we are talking about your parents," Emi said.

"They have absolutely lost it," I said, locking my seat belt.

Emi glanced over her shoulder as she backed out of the driveway. "What happened?"

"They think the dog can kill me."

"Biting or barking?"

"They think I can get sick from the dog licking my face," I said

"Well can you?" Emi looked over at me. She had braided her hair into one plait from her temples to her shoulders. There was an apple-green ribbon running through the braid.

"How can you even ask me that?"

"Simple: I don't know." She turned left at Hibiscus Lane.

"I'm sure that Dr. Braden would have told me if I couldn't keep Ajax."

"Did he tell you other things you couldn't do?" Emi asked. When she turned her head, her braid swung back against her shoulder.

"He said no drinking, no ear piercing, no tattoos, no contact sports, no drugs, blah, blah, blah."

"But he didn't mention dogs?"

"No."

"Did he know you had a dog?"

"Yes."

"So you can figure having a dog is okay." Her face was unsmiling.

"But my parents are talking about getting rid of him."

"Did they say they were going to get rid of him?"

I felt like a third grader being questioned by the school principal. "No."

"Then we can go to *The Sassafras Shop* in peace."

"Yes."

"Rell, you know they won't get rid of the dog." Emi sounded annoyed.

"You're right," I told Emi. I didn't believe it, but, I didn't want to fight with her, too, so I said, "Nice ribbon," pointing to her braid.

"Isn't it cool? I'm going to get silk cords at *The Sassafras Shop*. Sara told me they're marked down 75%."

We turned down Ilima Road toward Jefferson Park. Vans lined the street, and there were families unloading coolers and beach chairs. A couple of boys in Little League uniforms swung their bats as they walked.

"Great dog." Emi pointed to a Great Dane pup with surgical tape on its ears.

"I wonder if he'll give his owners some deadly virus," I said.

"I thought we were finished with cancer today," Emi said.

"Sorry," I said. "I didn't know it was such an issue."

Emi tapped on the steering wheel. "It's a never-ending issue with you," she said.

"For once you're right," I said. "It is never ending."

"Look, Rell, all I want to do is go to *The Sassafras Shop*, buy some ribbon, and try on a few toe rings. I don't want to hear about cancer today."

I decided that her braid looked stupid. It made her ears stick out like sugar bowl handles.

"Can't we just go shopping like we used to?" Emi looked over at me. "You know, I drag you around, you complain, and then we get something to eat."

"Sure," I said. "I wouldn't want to spoil your day."

"What was that supposed to mean?"

"Just what I said. I wouldn't want to ruin your precious day."

Emi turned down Marsh Road and pulled over and turned off

the engine. "It is so awful that I would want one day without cancer?" she said.

"My mother says that wanting is good," I said. "It builds character."

"I don't want to fight with you, Rell."

"Are we fighting?" I asked oh-so-innocently.

"Yes, we are," she said.

"Okay," I said. "You want one day without cancer. I'd like a whole life without it. Do you think you can arrange that?"

She didn't answer.

"Of everyone, I thought you would understand me," I said.

"Rell, I'm sick of everything being about you. Your life. Your dog. Your parents, and your damn cancer."

"Like your clothes, your movie stars, your newest boyfriend?"

"Your cancer is beginning to piss me off," she said.

"That's it. I got cancer just to piss you off."

"Stop with the pity party, Rell. You don't have cancer anymore!"

I shook my head. "You don't get it." Right then I wanted to drag her into the cancer ward at Stanhope. Maybe then she would get it.

"You don't ever 'not have cancer anymore,'" I said. "You haven't listened to a word I've said."

"I haven't listened? Let me see. What don't I know about?" Emi counted on her fingers. "There's the chemo IVs, the radiation burns, the dry mouth, the rashes, the nightmares, and the night sweats. I even know that your damn pubic hairs itched when they grew back in." She looked over at me. "Did I miss anything, Rell? Because if I did, it's not because you didn't tell me—you told me every last detail over and over again."

"Are you through?" I asked.

"No." Tears dripped down Emi's cheek. "I'm sick of you playing the cancer card. You wear it, like that wig." She sobbed. "Like it was some kind of merit badge."

"You're jealous of the attention I get," I said. "For once it's me, not you, who's getting attention. I'm the one with a boyfriend. I finally have my own life, and you're pissed."

"You've uncovered the truth, Rell. I want cancer, too, so I can have my own pity party."

"It's true."

"God, you are so self-centered. Tell me one thing that happened to me while you were in San Francisco. I dare you."

I couldn't think of anything that fast.

"You can't."

"I'm thinking," I said.

"You don't remember because all you think about is you. You, you, and you.

"So tell me what happened."

"First of all, I tried out for the volleyball team and didn't make it. I made it to the last cut, but then they picked Jacqueline Maldonado instead of me. I emailed you about it, but you never mentioned it."

"Excuse me," I said. "I was busy fighting for my life."

"Rell, the Cancer Queen." Her voice cracked. "You were also too busy to remember my birthday."

"I was sick," I blurted out.

"Too sick to remember your almost–best friend's friend."

There it was. "You're my best friend," I said.

"Next to LB."

"You are my best friend, Emi."

"I'm your only friend," she said.

"What's that supposed to mean?"

"The only one who will tell you the truth about yourself," she said.

"With friends like you, who needs enemies?"

"Great response, Rell. Did you remember that from sixth grade?"

"Why can't you get it? I almost died."

"That's it," Emi said. "I hereby resign from the Poor-Little-Rell Club."

"Nate cares about me. He understands me."

"I was waiting for that," Emi said.

"He listens to me."

"He feels sorry for you," she said.

"You're mad because I have a boyfriend and you don't," I said.

"Right. I'm just dying to be with your tight-assed Tiger Boy."

"I can't believe you're being so mean," I said.

Emi didn't answer. We'd said things to each other that we couldn't take back. It was as if we had both crossed a bridge and there was no turning back.

"I'm going home," I said. I opened the door and started to get out.

"Don't be stupid. It's at least three miles."

"I'd rather be alone," I said.

"Stop it, Rell," Emi said.

I got back in the car.

"Rell, do you remember when you would call me from Stanhope and we would talk about all the things we were going to do when you came home?"

"Uh-huh."

"I thought we were really going to do them."

"Me, too," I said.

Now it was me who was crying. "You're right about me," I said. "Maybe I did get caught up with myself." Although, I still thought I had every right to.

"Friends forever?" Emi asked and she held up her pinky. "Friends forever," I said, and we hooked our pinkies together. "And

Emi," I said. "I didn't me forget your birthday. I was going to send you a Stanhope Teddy Bear from the gift shop, but I forgot."

"It's okay," she said.

"No, it isn't," I said. "But I promise to make it up to you. Maybe I could find that hula dancer on the postcard that Sara sent me and have him give you a special performance." I thought that by saying it we could move past it. But I could see her face, it was a mistake.

"Emi," I said. "I'm sorry."

"Right," she said.

"You know how it is when your team gets to the finals, and then you lose?"

"So?"

"It's kind of like that when you have cancer. Well, not exactly, but I can't explain it."

"Like LB made the team and I didn't."

I was getting nowhere. "You know what, you're right," I said. "I won't talk about LB, or anything that happened at Stanhope."

"Deal," she said. "We'll shop till we drop and then hit Maui Taco for lunch."

I didn't think it was a good idea to shop. Fighting made me tired, and I didn't want to deal with anything else that morning. There was Emi, my parents, and taking my wig off in front of Nate. I was tired, and wanted to go home. "Nate's coming over about five," I said.

"So? I'll get you home by three."

"I'm okay for the mall, but I can't handle lunch, too. I'll need a nap if I want to go out tonight." She knew how hard it was for me to make it through the day without one.

"Dear Nate." She said his name like it was a fatal disease. "You know what? Why don't I take you home right now and you can sleep all day for your precious Nate."

"Emi."

"Forget shopping," she said. "You'd be no fun anyway."

"Emi, I need you to be my best friend." It came out all wrong.

"I don't want to be needed, Rell."

"Let me explain," I said.

"I don't have the time. I've got a whole store of sales waiting for me."

I opened the car door again and started to get out.

"You're honestly walking home?"

I shook my head.

She didn't try to stop me. "Don't get too tired," she said.

I got out of the car and walked to the corner. Before I crossed the street, I waited a few seconds. I was sure that Emi would drive by and offer to take me home. But she didn't.

I walked slower because I thought that she circled the block. I knew she would be swinging around the corner and get me. But she didn't.

At the traffic light, I brushed imaginary hair away from my face, and turned around to check the cars behind me. Emi's wasn't there.

I squinted at oncoming cars. No Emi. I thought she might be waiting for me in the Safeway lot. That was her last chance. When she wasn't there, I cut through the Chevron lot and took a shortcut to the beach.

I climbed over the chain next to the "No Trespassing" sign, and walked down the dirt path. The bougainvillea hedge had grown over it, like a canopy of colored petals. It was like walking through a tunnel, and at end of the tunnel was the Pacific Ocean, the waves, the sand, and the sun.

The sand was hot, and the sun was intense. I walked on the wet sand because it was cooler, and I watched windsurfers bounce through the waves. Lime green, pink, and lemon yellow sails.

As I walked, I popped jellyfish under my feet. I stopped to pet a sand-covered dog, and I smiled at anyone I saw. A fisherman was sitting in an aluminum tube chair, guarding his line. There were kids in the water, boogey boarding, and lines of oil-slick tourists baking on their towels.

I remembered when Emi and would go boogey boarding at Kailua Beach. We would build sand castles on the beach.

On her thirteenth birthday, Emi's parents threw her a '50s theme party at a bungalow across the canal. On her sixteenth birthday, they threw her a spa night slumber party, and sixteen girls slept over her house. We painted each other's toenails, gave each other facials, and played a game where we paired up, and one of the girls was blindfolded, and she put makeup on her partner according to the directions we all shouted out.

Before I got sick, Emi slept over at my house a lot. She thought it was cool for me to be an only child—no hand-me-down clothes, no yelling at dinner, no brothers or sisters who squealed on you. I thought it was cool at her house, where I could get lost in the crowd.

I thought about buying Emi a bucket of spa stuff for a birthday present. Or maybe getting Sara and Faye together and having a party, but that didn't seem right. I thought that maybe my mother and I could take her to some fancy place for lunch, but that wouldn't do it either.

As I walked, the sun got hotter. I got more tired. My purse strap dug into my shoulder and sweat trickled from under my wig. I scavenged through my purse for my cell phone, but I'd forgotten it in my room. *If I hadn't left in such a huff,* I thought, *I would have had it with me.*

I rested in the shade of an ironwood tree for a while. I couldn't imagine how I forgot Emi's birthday. I had photos of her all over my room. I talked about her all the time.

"Charlie!" A pregnant woman lumbered to her feet. "Charlie, stop." She was yelling at a little boy who was running after an Arctic tern.

When the bird took flight, the boy burst into tears, and his mom scooped him up into her arms and cradled him to her chest. "It's okay, honey," she soothed him. "It's okay." She brushed the sand from his legs and kissed his feet. "You're mommy's brave little hunter."

Mom to the rescue.

A gray-haired couple sitting next to me watched the whole thing, too. They smiled at me. I smiled back. At the beach, life was simple.

What's life? Life's a magazine. How much does it cost? One dollar? What's one dollar? Life. What's life? Life's a magazine.

I had two more miles to walk, and was beginning to wonder if I could make it.

CHAPTER EIGHT

When I got home, Mom was standing at the kitchen sink. Her hands were buried in suds.

"Hi, Mom," I said. "I'm back."

"I didn't know you'd left," she said. "Funny, I didn't hear you say goodbye."

"Sorry. I should have said goodbye."

She rinsed off a crystal goblet and placed it upside down with the others on the dish rack. "I didn't hear you, Rell," she said. That was Mom's way of telling me I missed the point, and hadn't said the right thing.

"I'm sorry for what I said." I thought I gave her the apology she was looking for. "But I love Ajax."

"It's not only what you said it, but how you said it." She wiped her hands on the towel. "Your father and I are not your school friends, Rell. If you want to talk to them that way, that's your business, but I'm your mother and I won't tolerate it. And this tantrum of storming out of the house is not like you."

"I love Ajax," I said. That's when I noticed that he wasn't around. "Where is Ajax?"

"He's in the garage," she said. "I just gave him a bath."

"Did you clean him up to take him to the Humane Society?"

"I bathed him because he was dirty and I'm the only one around here who does it."

Score one for mom.

I heard Ajax scratching at the back door. "Can I let him in?"

"He's still wet."

"I'll dry him."

"No." That was another power play for Mom.

"Did Dr. Braden call?" I asked.

"Yes," she said. "He explained that if you were a veterinarian, there would be a health risk, but having a dog as a house pet isn't an issue."

"So Ajax stays," I said.

"Ajax stays. But I still want you to be more cautious."

I wanted to move the conversation right along, past the dog, so she didn't have any second thoughts. "Are you having company for dinner?" I gestured toward the crystal drying in the rack.

She nodded. "Dad's managers are coming over to talk about the Hilo job," she said.

"Does that mean he's not going to Guam?"

She shrugged.

I knew better than ask any more questions. Then she asked me if Emi and had a good time, and if I was hungry.

I wanted to scream out in big, bold letters. No, I am not hungry. Instead I told her that Emi and I ate lunch at a Thai restaurant. It was one more lie on my path to hell.

"Did you go to that new restaurant next to video store?"

"Uh-huh."

"What time is Nate picking you up?" she asked.

"About five," I said.

"I think you should take a nap, Rell. Going out all morning, then going out with Nate, it may be too much for one day."

"You're right, Mom," I said. For once I agreed with her. I was exhausted from walking the beach. "Could you wake me up at about three-thirty?" The idea of lying in bed with the ceiling fan cooling me off was very appealing.

"Sure will," she said, and, precisely at three-thirty, Mom jolted me awake. "My God, Rell. Look at yourself!" She pointed to the dresser.

I sat up and stared at the red-lobster face in the mirror.

"You're burned to a crisp!"

No denying it. I was glowing.

"Rell, you know you have to be careful about being in the sun. How could you do this to yourself?" Mom asked.

I didn't plan it, Mom.

"How many times have I told you to wear sunscreen? Every day, no matter what." She grabbed my chin and looked at my face. "What did you and Emi do? Lie on the beach instead of go shopping?"

"Plans change, Mom."

I watched in the mirror as she poked my cheek with her finger. It left a bloodless white imprint. "Do you have any of that prescription cream for radiation burns left?" she asked.

"I think so." I got to my bathroom before my mother got in there, and snooped around. Ajax followed behind me, and tried to stick his head under the sink.

"Go away, boy," I said.

He thought I was playing, hunched down and ran around in circles.

"Not now, Ajax."

"Ajax," Mom yelled, and the dog jumped on the bed, right next to her.

"Get down," she said, and the dog jumped down, cut across my desk, then he leaped back on the bed on to my mother's lap.

Suddenly the whole thing seemed hilarious to me. My glowing face, Ajax jumping on the bed, my mother on the verge of a meltdown. It was like a cheap movie. Then I remembered Dad doing his impersonation of the drunken limbo dancer in the movie *Sixteen Summers.*

That was when it hit me—nobody laughed in my house anymore. There were a lot of oh-my-poor-baby smiles, but there wasn't any knee-slapping, belly-belching laughing.

The movie *Sixteen Summers* was a riot. I wished I could have starred in that movie. I'd be the preacher's daughter who had sex with the pool guy, who was really a detective hired by the preacher to watch his daughter.

I handed my mother the burn cream.

"Rell, you get me so upset."

I knew what was coming. Whenever mom told me I got her upset, I knew that I was in for one of her I'm-trying-to-be-the-best-cancer-mothers-I-can-be lectures.

"Rell, do you remember Dr. Braden explaining about how you are at high risk for skin cancer?"

"Yes, Mom."

You tend to listen when doctors talk to you about cancer and dying.

"Rell, you're not like other girls anymore."

I am like other girls, Mom.

"I worry when I see you do things like this." She stroked the cream over my face.

I pictured the surfer-boy neighbor in *Sixteen Summers.* He was the guy the preacher thought his daughter was playing around with. His name was Rex. In the opening scene, he got knocked off a wave and his board shorts got pulled way down.

"This burn could have been prevented with some common sense," Mom said.

Rex had a butt that looked like two plump pears.

Mom worked the cream on my shoulders and neck. "Rell, I try so hard not to be afraid for you."

Try harder, Mom.

"Last week a student of mine was diagnosed with breast cancer. She's nineteen."

I don't need to know this, Mom.

"Of course, it has nothing to do with you, but every time I see her I get reminded of cancer."

And every time I take a shower and see a fourteen-inch scar down my chest, and every time I take off my wig, and every time this, and every time that, I get reminded, too.

I wanted to disappear into the limbo party in *Sixteen Summers*. I wanted to sprawl across the sand with some six-foot-three lifeguard pouring Mai Tais down my throat.

The truth was that I never got drunk in my life. Not falling down, puking, gut-wrenching, passed-out drunk. My mother just couldn't appreciate how lucky she was to have a kid like me.

"Rell, we've been through a lot this year," Mom said.

Excuse me, Mom, but I think that I'm the one who went through it all.

"I just don't want to have to do it again. I don't know if I can handle another bout of cancer."

Right, Mom, your cancer.

If cancer came back, it would be all mine and it would be different. The first time around I didn't know what to expect. The second, I would know what was coming. I used to watch the second-go-round kids at Stanhope. I couldn't imagine how they did it. Some of them acted like zombies, and just went through treatment like they weren't there. Others acted like athletes in training for a fight. Some gave up. I'm not sure what I would do.

"I love you, Rell," Mom said. "You are my beautiful star." Then she cried, and, one more time, I felt like I had to protect her from my cancer, and I resented it.

"Rell, you've got to promise me you'll take better care of your-self."

"I will, Mom."

I let her rock me in her arms, but I kept thinking about the preacher's daughter. At the end of the movie, she went to a party with the surfer guy who lived next door, and she slugged down a can of beer in less than thirty seconds. I wondered if that was humanly possible.

While Mom was holding me, I held my breath and imagined a beer flowing down my throat. Maybe it could be done.

"Where is Nate taking you on your date?" she asked me.

"It's not a date, Mom."

"Well, whatever it is you call it these days. What time is he coming?"

"He's coming at five. I told you."

In the movie, the preacher's daughter almost died because she let the drunken surfer boy drive her home, and they got into an accident.

"You are a beautiful woman, Rell." She smiled. "Even if you look like a Waikiki tourist right now."

"Thanks, Mom."

"What are you going to wear tonight?" She walked over to my closet and held up my blue-green dress. "This color would make you look less red," she said.

"Good idea, Mom," I said, knowing that I was going to wear my jeans and my purple lace top.

When I put my jeans on, they hung down on me. I put my hands where my hips used to be. I had lost so much weight, I didn't have hips anymore. I didn't have a chest or a backside either. Basi-cally, I had the figure of a ten-year-old boy.

I wore my silver dolphin earrings and slathered sand-beige foundation all over my face and neck. Most of the sunburn was covered. *Smile,* I told myself. *Let your "glowing" personality show through.*

Then I sprayed myself with vanilla perfume because *Seventeen* said guys think vanilla is the sexiest smell there is. Personally, I think it has to do with the smell of fresh-baked cookies and their mothers, but I wasn't going there.

The front doorbell rang. I was all ready, except for a final tug on my wig. The bell rang again.

"Is anyone going to get that?" Dad asked, which was Dad-speak for, "Rell, Nate's here, get the door."

When I answered the door a dark figure with spiked black hair, wide cheekbones, and duct tape over his mouth appeared. It was Nate.

His eyes shouted at me, "Go ahead, ask me what the duct tape is doing across my mouth."

I acted like there was nothing unusual about how he looked. "I'm going to say good night to my folks," I said. "I'll tell them you said hello."

When I got back I asked Nate, "Is this a new version of man talk?"

He shook his head.

"Is this a game?"

He nodded.

"What kind of game?"

As we walked to the car, he handed me an index card marked "Number One." Then he made a flipping motion with his hands. The back of the card read, "You can find your dreams if you follow the clues."

"What dreams?" I asked.

He pointed again, stabbing the card with his finger.

"Okay, I'll play," I said. "Dreams. Dreams at the end of a rainbow? Are we going to Rainbow's for chicken *katsu?*"

He shook his head.

"Dreams? Dreams like fortunes? We're going to Chinatown to get our fortune told."

This time he vigorously shook his head.

I climbed in his truck and he closed the door behind me. As we drove away, I wondered if it was legal for him to drive with duct tape across his mouth.

He pointed to card number two on the dashboard. I read it out loud. "To follow your dream, you must take one step after another."

"Okay, Nate, what is this?"

He turned toward me. He looked like he was smiling. His eyes narrowed, and under the duct tape I detected an upward curve of his mouth.

"One step after another," I repeated. "It's not the marathon, that's for sure." I fidgeted with the card. "Night hiking?"

He kept his eyes on the road.

"Are we going hiking?"

Another no.

"Maybe a walk. Honolulu Time Walk? The Ghost Tour?"

I was wrong again.

I thought out loud. "One step after another, but not a hike and not a walk. A street? A road? A road less traveled? The yellow brick road? The road to where? Where in the world is Carmen San Diego?" I turned to Nate. "That's it! We're flying to San Diego."

He laughed a muffled laugh and pointed to the glove box where, buried among half-eaten Lifesavers and parking stubs for Honolulu General Hospital, was card number three, stuck to a crumpled up Power Bar wrapper.

I peeled the card off the wrapper and read, "Tonight you will receive a gift that was inspired by dreams."

I looked around in his truck. There was an old milk crate

jammed in the cubby behind my seat that was overflowing with basketball shoes, stinky towels, dirty T-shirts, and probably last week's gym clothes. "Dreams? This truck could inspire nightmares."

Nate shrugged.

We were headed into the first Pali tunnel. Between the first and second tunnel was a view of the windward side from Kailua to the North Shore. It was my favorite view on the island.

Nate jabbed the card with his finger.

"Yes, sir." I snapped an exaggerated salute. "This is my dream that's coming true, not yours," I said. "Fat chance of any of your dreams coming true, buster." He took his hands off the wheel, clasped them in prayer and leaned toward me in a fake plea.

"Hey! Pay attention to the road!" I pointed to the car in front of us. "Fooling around on the Pali make me nervous."

Right outside the second tunnel was an emergency parking lot with a phone, a first-aid kit, and a bench. Nate pulled over into the lot. He reached inside his pocket and handed me another card. It said, "From now on I will only go where you tell me to go. You can continue to play or give up and never find your dream."

"I'll play," I said.

He handed me card number five. "The memory of this city's lights brings the islander home again."

"Honolulu," I said.

By the eighth card I was standing next to the hula girl statue at the Aloha Tower Marketplace. Nate still had the duct tape over his mouth, apparently unbothered by the stares of tourists.

One old guy in a porkpie hat and brown plaid shorts called over to Nate. "You look like you're in training for being married."

"Stop it, Harry." The man's wife jabbed his belly, setting off a tidal wave of fat rippling across his shirt—a rayon Aloha shirt that matched her hibiscus *mu'u mu'u.*

Nate gave Harry a thumbs-up.

By the time I read the last card, I was in front of the cash register at the Blue Hawaii Bookstore. The last card said, "Hand this to the clerk and claim a gift for Estrella DeMello.

The clerk exchanged the card for a wrapped hardcover book. The gift tag had Nate's handwriting. "To my Beautiful Star, From Nate."

"You know what my name means."

Nate took a sweeping bow.

I gently pulled off the wrapping paper to uncover *The Dream of Light: A Path through the Grand Canyon* by Makana Johns. "I've wanted this book for so long." I threw my arms around him and kissed the duct tape across his lips.

As I leafed through the book, he peeled the tape off his mouth. Sliver strands of adhesive stuck to what looked like an instant rash across his face.

"You okay?" I asked.

"I think so." He patted his mouth with the back of his hand.

I stood on my tiptoes and gave him another kiss.

"Ouch."

"Ruin the moment," I said, pretending to be hurt. "Pure romance spoiled by a mouth pansy."

"Mouth pansy?" Nate put his arm around me, dipped me back and kissed me. The second he let go, he put his hand over his mouth. "Jeez, that stings."

"You know, for a smart guy, you've got zero common sense."

I wanted to give Nate a big Santa Claus hug and cover him with hundreds of kisses.

"This is the best gift I ever got," I said.

He beamed with Man Pride.

"Are you ready for what's next?" he asked.

"There's more?"

"You bet."

The more was more fries, more ketchup, and more beef in your burgers. We ate at Bruddah's Grill at the end of Aloha Tower pier at a table overlooking the harbor.

The SS *Independence* cruise ship was berthed next to us. It was lit up like a birthday cake with strung white lights for candles, and red and blue streamers for frosting.

Halfway through our meal, I felt a low-pitched rumble. The pier vibrated; the ship's horn blasted. Little girls in ti-leaf skirts danced hula on the dock, and right on cue, a helicopter showered the cruise ship with plumeria blossoms. It was just like in the movies. I reached for Nate's hand and braided my fingers into his.

He handed me a napkin with his other hand. "You've got ketchup on your cheeks."

My wonderfully unromantic Nate.

Our waitress refilled our water glasses, then rested the pitcher on her hip. "Are you on vacation?" she asked.

"Yes," Nate answered. "We're from San Francisco."

"You may want to stick around." She lifted her pitcher in the direction of Diamond Head. "The Hilton puts on a fireworks show in fifteen minutes."

"Thanks," he said.

I wanted to turn that night into a nine-by-twelve glossy photo, framed in gold and forever untouched. I twirled a vandah orchid from my plate between my fingers. "Thanks," I said. "The game, the ship, the book. It's all perfect."

Nate held my hand tighter. "I hope you get to go on your trip."

"No hoping about it," I said. "We're going just as soon as we figure out a way to pay for it."

Nate looked at his watch. "What about the Make-A-Wish Foundation? I bet they'd pay for LB's trip. Maybe yours, too."

"Maybe hers," I said. "But not mine, I've had it with being a cancer kid," I said. "Even if my best friend doesn't believe me," I muttered. "I'll be sixteen this summer. I can get a job at The Great Outdoors at Ala Moana. They give their employees a 30% discount, so I can buy all the stuff that LB and I will need."

"You're serious about this."

"You bet," I said. "LB found a tour company that might hire us to take pictures."

"Do you think she'll be able to handle the hiking?" Nate looked at his watch again.

"I hope so."

"You never told me what LB stands for." Nate motioned over the waitress.

"Lightbulb Head," I whispered it. "I know it sounds cruel, but it isn't really. Her real name is Elizabeth. Tess first called her 'Lightbulb Head' because when her hair fell out, her head almost glowed. Then it got shortened to Light Bulb, then LB, and LB stuck."

The waitress was busy with other customers. Nate looked at his watch again. "Rell, why don't you order dessert for us? Get me the coconut ice cream in the chocolate shell," he said. "I've got to go back and feed the parking meter." He stood up to go.

"Why don't we just go to Bubbie's for ice cream?" I suggested.

"You don't mind missing the fireworks?"

"We could make our own at the beach." I winked.

I couldn't believe I actually said that! What a jerky thing to say.

"You got it, babe," Nate said.

Chapter Nine

We never stopped at Bubbie's that night. We drove the long way home, by Sandy Beach and through Waimanalo. Oldies played on the radio, and Nate held my hand as he drove.

Nate pulled in to the same parking spot he did on the night he first kissed me. We walked down the same beach path. The sky was cloudless, and the beach was deserted. It was just like the first time, except this time, our arms rested on each other's waists. This time he carried a straw mat rolled under his arm, this time the waves were stronger, the surf louder, the tide higher, and the kisses more frenzied.

Nate lost control, and the perfect night was ruined.

"Stop!" I pushed him away.

He looked at me as if he didn't know what was wrong,

"I thought your mouth was hurting from the duct tape," I said.

"Not anymore." He put his arm around me again.

I scooted back on the mat and pulled my knees up to my chest. "Lots of stars out tonight," I said, staring up at the sky.

Nate lowered his hand to my waist and nuzzled the back of my neck. I felt like he was Ajax, digging his snout around my neck for a biscuit that wasn't there.

"It looks like the tide is coming in," I said.

"Uh-huh." Nate kissed behind my ears.

"The moon's full." I took in a deep breath.

He didn't stop kissing me.

If he pushes his head any higher up my ear, he's going to knock off my wig.

I had visions of it floating out to sea like a soggy mongoose sprawled on a wave.

"Don't." I pushed him away.

"What's wrong?"

Lots of things. He didn't stop. He worked his kisses up my neck. I was sure my wig was tilted on my head like a French sailor in a drug-bust movie. I tugged at it, thinking Nate would figure out to leave it alone. But he put his arm around me again and coaxed my head on his chest. He was touching my wig!

"My wig!" I pulled away.

"I'm sorry."

I wanted to follow a sand crab right down a hole and hide forever.

"I didn't mean anything," Nate said.

"It's okay." I drew my knees back to my chest. I cradled them with my arms, and rested my chin on my knees. For a few minutes, we didn't talk.

"What's your hair look like under there?" Nate asked.

I wanted to say "like a chemo patient's just out of treatment," but only LB would get that joke. I looked at his face—his almond eyes, his wonderful smile, and I couldn't be mad. "It looks like a newborn Chinese baby's," I said.

He laughed. "So it sticks out everywhere."

"And it's short."

"It can't be shorter than Mitsu Fujimoto's," he said.

"Mitsu's hair is styled. Mine is growing in."

"Could I see it?" he asked.

"No."

"You've got to take it off sometime."

"No."

"Who's out here to see?" he asked.

You.

"Come on, Rell." He rubbed the back of my neck. "It's okay."

"My hair is stubby."

"It's probably not as bad as you think."

"And parts of it look like duck down. You know, fuzzy"

"I heard fuzzy is in."

I slipped my hands under the elastic edge of my wig. *What if he laughs at me?*

"You want some help?" Nate asked.

"No!"

"Sorry."

Now I hurt his feelings.

I lifted the wig straight up, the whole time I was thinking what a dumb thing it was to do. "When the fuzz falls off, my real hair grows it," I jabbered. When I get nervous, I jabber.

The wig was off. *Now I have to look at him.*

"Well?" I asked.

He didn't answer. He just sat there. He was supposed to say, "It looks great, Rell," or "Good for your, Rell," or smile, or clap, or do something positively wonderful. But all he did was look at me.

"Well?" I repeated.

"Give me a minute."

I grabbed my wig and started to put it back.

"Don't." Nate put his hand over mine and stopped me. "It doesn't look that bad," he said.

That bad. How bad? Like a train wreck bad or lousy hair cut bad?

"I'm putting it back on," I said.

He tightened his grip on my arm. "It's not ugly. Honest."

"Wow! I can't handle all the compliments."

"You look fine, Rell." Nate cupped my face in his hands and lifted it. "Look at me, Rell," he whispered.

I closed my eyes.

He kissed my cheek, my closed eyelids, and my forehead. "It's okay, Rell." Then he kissed the top of my patchy, bald head.

"How can you…?"

"You're beautiful, Rell," he said, and kissed me again, and he leaned me back on the mat, and rolled on top of me.

"Stop!"

"What did I do now?"

This was the other half of his game, I thought. Get me to take off my wig, humiliate me, then have sex with me.

"You're a real asshole," I said.

"Forty bucks for a book. I waste my whole day making up stupid index cards, and I'm an asshole."

"You don't understand."

"I'm trying to."

"You have no idea."

"You're right about that, Rell. You said this was the best night of your life, the best present ever got and you're the one who said you wanted to make fireworks at the beach."

"I didn't mean that kind of fireworks," I said. "It was stupid." I cringed. "It was a stupid thing to say, and I'm sorry."

"Okay," Nate said. "You're coming in loud and clear now."

"And then you made me take off my wig—"

"Wait, I didn't make you do anything. I asked you."

"I did it because you wanted me to."

Nate laughed. "Well, that doesn't always work, does it. Wigs. Yes. Fireworks. No."

"Sorry," I said, and reached for his hand. "Sometimes I get scared."

"Welcome to the real world, Rell. It's scary."

"I was afraid of letting you see me without my wig."

"And you did it. Now it's over."

Another cut-and-dry mathematical formula from Nathan Lee: Fear of taking off a wig minus taking it off, equals move on.

"And you think I'm going to have sex with you, so I can do it and then it'll be over?"

"Jeez, Rell. I have no idea how your head works."

"You just wanted to have sex with me," I said.

"Let me get this straight. You think I made you take off your wig, so I could have sex with you?"

It sounded lame when he said it. "I want to be regular again," I said.

"Constipation got you down?" It was a mean thing to say.

"Forget it," I said.

"I'm not a mind reader, Rell."

"All right, I'll try to explain," I said. "There was a first grader who left Stanhope about three months before I did. She finished her treatment and she was really healthy and she went back to school." I looked at Nate. "You sure you want to hear this?"

"No, I'm an asshole, who asks questions just to get you to have sex." He was more angry than I thought.

"One day the girl told her teacher that her father was beating her just so she could get special attention. It was a lie—she was afraid of being a regular kid again, not special."

"That doesn't make any sense," Nate said.

"I told you that you wouldn't understand."

"Rell, this girl was in first grade. You're fifteen."

"It doesn't matter," I said. "She couldn't move past her cancer. It's not that easy."

"I know," he said.

"You don't know," I said.

"Well, I know I'm not afraid of being normal," he said.

"Are you ever afraid?" I asked.

"Sometimes."

"Of what?"

"When I was at St. Luke's, Samuel Larsen came to talk to us."

"The movie director?"

"Yeah."

I felt a chill down my back. I realized that for the first time in months there was a breeze on my head.

"Larsen said that great movies always have great characters"

"There's big news."

"He said the key to creating great characters it to remember that all people are afraid. It's the way they deal with their fear that makes them who they are."

"And?"

"There's the public way—the way we show everyone else. It's how we pretend to be brave. Then there are the private times, when we're alone an we have to face fear head on."

"This coming from a guy who makes movies about car chases?" I said.

"But he makes sense, Rell." He waved his hands in the air as he explained. "Don't you get it? Some people pretend to be brave by becoming bullies or athletes, or driving fast cars. Some people take drugs or write poetry, but in some way, we're all trying to drive away the fear."

"So all I need to do is to drive a fast car and write shitty poetry?"

"All you have to do is figure out what you're afraid of and deal with it."

"Is that all, oh great Chinese philosopher?"

"Rell, do you think your cancer will come back?"

You're not supposed to ask questions like that. It's not polite.

"My doctor says it's normal to be afraid of a relapse," I answered.

"Nice lateral pass, Rell," Nate said. "Let's try again. Do you, or does your doctor, think that your cancer will come back?"

"The doctors don't talk like that," I said. "They talk about survival rates after five years. It's all numbers to them."

"Are yours good?" Nate wanted another mathematical formula.

"My numbers are good," I said. "The event-free survival rate after five years is 84%."

"Then your odds are good."

Not if you're in the other 16%.

"What are you afraid of?" I asked him.

"That I'll waste one minute of my life."

Emi was right; Nate was too intense.

That night Nate and I didn't fall into passionate lovemaking, but in some way we got closer. Trust wasn't the right word, comfortable wasn't it either. Maybe we opened up parts of ourselves that were secret before.

On the ride home that night, my wig was in my lap. I twirled strands of it between my fingers. Without my wig on, I felt lighter, freer, like I'd taken off a mask

Nate and I were singing along with the radio when the pain hit—a sharp stab at the base of my skull. I got those pains at Stanhope, too—headaches that sliced through my head like a jagged heated blade. Within seconds, the pain was in the back of my eyes. My heart pounded. I felt nauseous. I breathed shallowly, to keep the pain from getting worse.

"Why'd you stop singing?" Nate looked over at me.

I pressed my hands to my temples, and was bent forward.

"You okay, Rell?"

"Bad headache," I said. I could hardly talk.

"Do you have medicine with you?"

"No."

"Should I take you to the hospital?"

"Home." I said. Each word set off a throbbing reaction.

"Should I pull over?"

"Home."

I made it home. Nate walked me to the door. Dad's managers were still in the dining room. I went to my room, straight to the medicine cabinet and downed two Tylenols with codeine.

It's an ordinary headache, I told myself. *The head bone is not connected to the cancer bone.* I laid on my bed as still as I could. *Headaches are not a symptom of Hodgkin's disease. Repeat, one hundred times.*

CHAPTER TEN

The next morning, Mom nudged me awake. "LB is on the phone," she said.

I looked at my clock. It was eight a.m. "Tell her I'll call her later."

"She's crying," Mom said.

I took the phone. "Hey, LB, what's up?" I tried to sound upbeat.

"I know it's early there, Rell, but I have to talk to you."

"Never too early to talk to you."

"I'm scared, Rell." She was sobbing.

"What's wrong?"

"I heard the nurses talking about a bone marrow test for me on Tuesday. I'm not scheduled for one until next month."

"Maybe it's a scheduling error," I said. "You know how things get mixed up at the lab."

"It's no mistake."

"There could be lots of reason for it," I said, although I knew none of them were good. "How's your weight?" I asked.

"I lost three pounds last week," she said. "But I wasn't eating much."

"What about your blood tests?"

"Doctor Lynch is running them again," she said.

"Has he stopped your treatment?"

"Yes."

Not the right answer. As soon as she said it, I knew she was in trouble.

LB had leukemia when she was two years old, but when it came back it was refractory—which meant it wouldn't respond to treatment. When I first got to Stanhope, she was on her last three months of standard treatment. When that failed, she had a bone marrow transplant, and when that failed they started her on an experimental "smart-bomb" treatment.

"Doctor Lynch called another doctor in to examine me. He's from Seattle," Rell said.

"Fred Hutch?"

"Uh-huh."

That was another part of having cancer. Your vocabulary included too many medical terms and you knew which cancer centers specialized in what. Fred Hutchinson was strong in leukemia research.

"LB," I said.

She was sobbing.

"LB."

She kept crying, and there was nothing I could do for her.

If I were at Stanhope, I knew I could get her to laugh. I could pop in a silly DVD, or go into my silly fool routine. Or I could sit next to her, and we could talk, and if she didn't want to talk, I could hold her hand.

"What did the doc from Fred Hutch say?" I asked.

"The usual. 'How are you feeling, young lady?'"

I could hear her sniffling.

"He read over my chart for a long time, then I saw him and Dr. Lynch talking at the nurses' station." She stopped to catch her breath. "Then they paged Dr. Braden, and the three of them talked."

"LB, let's think about what's happening." I tried to sound logical. "It might not be as bad as you're imagining."

"You know that's not true." Then, with a frightening calm, she said, "I'm going to die, Rell."

"Don't say that."

"Last night was the first time I believed it," she said. "I always knew it could happen, but I never believed it before."

"Stop it, LB. We've got to think. Did you ask Dr. Lynch why he stopped your treatment?"

"I didn't have to ask. I know why."

"You're just scared."

"Rell, they called my parents to come up this weekend."

"That makes sense. The guy from Fred Hutch probably wants to talk to them about a new treatment."

"I'm going to die, Rell."

I knew LB was probably right. But maybe, just maybe, the Fred Hutch doc *did* want to talk to them about a new treatment. Maybe all the tests she was having were to see if she were a good candidate for a new clinical trial. Maybe this, maybe that, but I knew she was right. She was probably going to die.

"LB, I could be there tomorrow, if you want me."

She laughed. "Superwoman Rell, flying across the ocean."

"I'm sure my mother would put me on the next plane," I said.

"I'm tired, Rell," she said.

I was scared. "You okay?" I asked.

"I've got to go, Rell.

"I love you, LB," I said.'

She never said it back. She always answered, "Right back at you, Rell."

I hung up and sat on my bed hugging my pillow. I knew LB was going to die, just like I'd known Tess was going to die. I'd watched Tess. She got tired and gave up. She wouldn't try one more treatment. It could have been the one that saved her life.

I wasn't going to let LB give up. If the doc from Fred Hutch gave her any chance at all, I wasn't going to let her die.

How could any regular kid understand that? Talking about dying at fifteen years old? Having to choose between being a guinea pig or dying sooner? Sooner, but with less poking and prodding, treatments, IVs, and surgery. How could a normal kid understand that sometimes a hospital was a better place to live than at home?

Hospitals were safe places. They had routines. I knew that at that very moment, the interns were starting their rounds at Stanhope. At eleven-thirty, the lunch carts would line the hall. Then the nurses would come to check vital signs. Later the docs would make their visits. Dinner came next, then the evening shift came on, and more vital signs were taken.

The night cleaning lady would come to my room at about seven o'clock at night. Her name was Mrs. Olszowy. She was from Poland.

The first think she did when she came in was to say, "This is just for you, Moon Beam," and she would put a piece of hard candy on my bed stand. She said the same thing to every patient.

While she cleaned, Mrs. Olszowy told me stories about her daughter, who was an honor student at Oakland High School. "Someday," she said, "she's going to be a doctor. Right here."

I missed Mrs. Olszowy. I missed the aides, and the nurses, and even the vampire techs. There was always someone around who asked how I was feeling, and the doctors were only a page away. And if I needed to talk to anyone, there were plenty of kids around who understood.

Every day was the same in the hospital, except when somebody died. When I was at Stanhope, I couldn't wait to come home. But when I got home, there were times I wanted to be back there. That was something Emi couldn't understand. And more than anyone else, I wanted her to understand, because I needed a friend to talk to about LB.

I was sure if I called her and told her LB was dying that Emi would come over, and she'd listen and we'd be best friends again.

I punched her number in my phone, but she didn't answer. I was sure she checked who was calling and didn't pick up.

I called her house. Kalani answered. He said he thought that Emi was in the carport and he'd go out to find her, but when he got back he said, "My dad said she went out with her friends. Are you supposed to meet her somewhere?"

I was sure that Emi was standing right next to him, mouthing, "Tell her I'm out."

"Never mind," I said. I convinced myself Emi wouldn't have understood anyway.

I had to do something to keep my mind off LB, so I started working on my homework. Mr. Meyers assigned us an eight-line poem to write for English class. I typed out one poem after another. They all ended up being about LB, and dying. It was pretty crappy, tear-jerking stuff that I deleted before anyone would see it.

Nothing was working. So I called Sara and asked her if she wanted to go to the movies. *The Tin Box* was playing at the mall.

"Sure," she said. Things were so easy with Sara.

I got dressed, put on my makeup according to Emi's directions, and put on my Hat-Hair wig. Then I took it off. "No wig," I said. I checked myself out in the mirror, and put the wig back on. Then I took it off again.

"No guts. No glory," I said.

I walked in the kitchen and asked my mother if she would drive me to the mall to meet Sara.

She picked up her purse and keys. "Ready?" she asked. She didn't flinch, and didn't mention my bald head.

Halfway to the mall, I said, "I've decided to go topless." I pointed to my head.

"I noticed."

"And I noticed you didn't say anything," I said.

"Not that I didn't want to."

"Don't ruin it, Mom," I said. "You're doing so well."

When she dropped me, off she gave me an especially big hug.

"Thanks, Mom," I said. "I love you."

She smiled and let me go.

I darted across the parking lot. The mall doors swung back like a curtain pulling back on a day time drama. I made eye contact with two old ladies walking out of Banana Republic. They halted their conversation, and stopped in their tracks. One of them smiled at me, one of those Oh-my-God-she-has-no-hair-she-must-have-cancer smiles.

I smiled back.

The clerk at the garden kiosk stopped watering her plants and stared at me. I wanted to go up to her and ask if I was the first bald girl she had ever seen, but I ran instead.

A moving target is harder to see.

Sara was waiting for me in front of the movie theatre. "Great look!" She spun me around and rubbed my scalp. "Great shaped head. Not a flat spot anywhere."

"Thanks, I think."

A couple of guys passed us. They elbowed each other and turned back, snickering. I felt embarrassed for Sara, like some of my cancer rubbed off on her.

"You need a dragon tattoo slinking across the bottom of your scalp," Sara said.

"Right. Just what I need, more attention," I said. "Besides, only you could pull off something like that."

Sara was dressed in a mauve gauze skirt and a smocked midriff top. She was wearing several ankle bands with brass antique-looking bells on them.

"They're Egyptian," she said. "I'm thinking of taking Middle Eastern dancing lessons—you know, with veils."

"You mean belly dancing?"

"It's more complicated than that."

I raised my eyebrows.

"It's cultural," she said.

Sara was the smartest person I knew. She had a perfect GPA, took Advanced Placement Physics and French, and won every science fair she was in. But you'd never know she was smart. She didn't have a lot of common sense.

"I'm even wearing Egyptian musk." She took out a vial from her purse and put it under my nose.

"Smells like a head shop," I said.

Sara dabbed a dot on the ten-dollar bill that she handed the guy in the ticket booth. "It'll make the booth smell great," she said to me.

Sara treated everyone as if they loved her. Why not? It was the way she thought of everyone.

We sat in seats halfway up the theatre in the absolute middle. I was sitting directly under a draft blowing on my head. I tugged my T-shirt over my chin, and curled down in my seat. I was cold and each time I heard someone cough, I worried about catching whatever virus they were spewing into the air.

After the show, Sara asked me if I liked the movie. I told her I did.

As we walked, she pointed to Tropical Freeze ice cream parlor. "So that was you having a good time? You jiggled your foot during the whole movie."

"It's a nervous habit."

"With your hands tucked under your armpits?"

"I was cold," I said.

"Why didn't you say something? We could have moved."

Because if I'd said something, I wouldn't be normal.

Tropical Freeze had a movie review board inside. Instead of stars, or thumbs up, customers put ice cream cone magnets next to the title of the movies. I gave *The Tin Box* two cones. Sara gave it four.

When I ordered my ice cream, the guy behind the counter said, "Nice hair." If his head weren't shaved, and his nails weren't painted black, I would have wondered if he were making fun of me.

Sara and I ate our ice cream at stools at the counter in front of the store window.

"What were the kids like in the hospital where you were?" she asked.

"Basic kids," I said, digging into my Lahaina Sundae.

"Did the little kids know they were dying?" She asked it in a matter-of-fact way while she piled her M&M toppings on the side of her plate.

She noticed me watching her make the pile.

"I like to eat the candy last," she said, and then she repeated, "Did the little kids know they were dying?"

"Some," I answered. "Some were too young to understand."

"Sad." Sara crossed her legs, when she did, the bells on her ankle bracelets tinkled. "Were any of them in gene therapy?"

"How do you know about gene therapy?" I couldn't believe someone who didn't have cancer even heard of the stuff.

"Remember me? Sara Reynolds, brain geek. When you got sick, I looked up Hodgkin's disease on the Internet." She licked her spoon. "I read everything there was to read at the National Institute of Health."

"You may know more than I do."

"I said I read it, it doesn't mean I understood what I read."

I wondered if she read anything about LB's kind of leukemia. "Did you read anything about leukemia?" I asked.

"Sure. Most of the lymphoma stuff was lumped in with leuke-mia."

"Did you ever hear of ANL?"

Sara could change from being absent-minded to being sharply focused in a second. She stared blankly out the window. Her eyes seemed to be scanning information stored in her brain. "Did you know they're working on a vaccine against Hodgkin's disease?" she said.

"Yeah, but what about ANL?"

"I don't remember anything specifically." Sara leaned over the counter, and banged on the store window.

Faye, Sharlene, and Emi were walking by. My best friend, Emi, was at the mall without me.

Sara motioned them in.

"Rell, you look fantastic." Faye rubbed the fuzz on my head with her fingers.

"It's a lot longer than I thought it was," Sharlene said.

"Look." I felt Faye pick my hair straight up. "You should spike it." She turned to Sharlene. "It would be wild in purple."

"My mother would love that," I said.

Emi was standing behind them. We looked at each other, and then she walked out of the store.

"We're going to see *The Tin Box*," Faye said.

"Sara and I just saw it." I wanted to make sure that it would get back to Emi that I wasn't sitting at home waiting for her to call me.

"What did you think?" Sharlene asked.

Sara gave it a thumbs up. But, I was distracted watching Emi standing in front of the shoe store with her back to me. She can't face me, I thought. Or maybe she's still mad.

That night I wrote Emi a three-page letter. Some of the ink floated in tears on the paper. After I read it, I ripped it up in to hundreds of ragged pieces and tossed them in the trash. Then I started a second letter that I never finished.

I'll see her at school, I thought. I'll talk to her then.

It was Sunday night, and I still had to write the eight-line poem. I stared at the computer screen and waited for inspiration. It didn't come. I pressed out the photo of Tess with my hand. "Got any ideas, Tess? Anything. It doesn't have to be serious."

I felt like one of the church aides kneeling in front of a statue waiting for it to come alive. "Anything, Tess. Anything at all."

Then I remembered a poem she'd written about cancer growing inside of her, and I typed out my own poem.

> *I Am a Weed*
> *by Estrella DeMello*
>
> *I was damaged and scarred*
> *And still I flourished*
> *Like a weed breaking through the sidewalk*
> *Not knowing I was strong.*
> *I raised my face to the sun,*
> *I grew a thick stem and thorns so sharp*
> *That no one could touch me.*
> *I grew on my own.*

CHAPTER ELEVEN

Monday morning came. To wear a wig or not to wear one, that was the question. Whether it was better to risk the smirks of fools or hide under my wig forever.

I opted for no wig. But my strategy called for distraction. I layered my five stubby eyelashes with mascara and stuffed my bra with gym socks.

I checked myself out in the mirror and pulled out the socks.

During breakfast I mentioned to Mom that I was thinking of going to school without my wig. "What do you think?" I asked.

She turned it around on me. "What do you think?" she asked.

"I'm not sure."

"How did you feel without it at the mall?"

"A guy at Tropical Freeze told me my hair was nice." I didn't mention his shaved head or black fingernails.

"You could bring it with you in case you change your mind," she said.

"I'm going to go for it," I said.

When Mom pulled up in front of school, she patted my hand. "You keep your chin up, your shoulders back, and you walk in there like you own the place." It was like she was ordering me into battle. "You are beautiful, Rell. Don't forget that."

"Thanks, Mom." She made me feel like Joan of Arc.

As corny as my mother's speech was, I wore her words like armor. But when I walked into school, the armor melted. I pictured kids throwing their hands over their eyes, running for cover, doors slamming, and Wanda Yamanaka screeching over the PA, "Rell DeMello took off her wig!"

I wanted to run away. I wanted to disappear—forever in limbo—somewhere between being normal and a cancer kid. But you had to die to get to limbo, and death wasn't an option, not at the front door of Kailua High School with the whole world watching.

Go for it, I told myself. I clasped my books to my chest and walked down the hall with my chin up. "Expand the space between your waist and your ribs when you walk. Walk from your thighs, not from your knees." I read that was the way to walk with confidence in *Seventeen* magazine.

The walls didn't crumble. There was no lightning. No floods. No floors opened up and swallowed me whole.

Boys straight ahead of me.

They walked right by. They didn't stare. No snickers, no backward glances. They didn't care. *But girls care,* I thought. They'd keep me the Girl With Cancer forever. They'd make us a couple: Cancer, King of the Prom, and his Homecoming Queen, Estrella DeMello.

Jennifer Oshima was walking straight at me. "Hi, Rell," she said. "Great hair."

Jennifer wasn't a fair test; she was a born-again Christian.

"How very wow!" from Deborah Misaki.

Deborah didn't count either. She did drugs.

I walked down the hall, hearing my mother's words echo in my head. It worked until I saw Emi. She looked at my wigless head. She didn't say a word. Nothing.

"You want to talk?" I asked.

She stopped, but didn't say anything.

"Emi, please."

"I have nothing to say."

"I'm sorry," I said. It seemed to me like I was apologizing to everyone.

A few kids jostled by us. Paul Cruz was one of them. "Looking sexy, Rell."

Emi rolled her eyes.

"Was that my fault, too?" I asked. "Did I tell Paul to say that?"

"No," she said.

"I told you I was sorry. What else can I do?"

Emi sighed. "Do you know what you're apologizing for?"

"I was selfish," I said. "But I needed to be."

"You got pretty good at it."

"Emi, when you're really sick, all you can think about is yourself."

She didn't say anything. Jack Flynn came over and handed Emi a biology lab workbook. He looked at me and said, "Good for you, Rell. That takes guts."

"One more time, Rell, the Heroic Cancer Survivor."

"Emi, it's not my fault I'm getting attention."

"You love it."

"Emi, I'm sorry I forgot your birthday, and that I forgot everything that was going on with you. But when you're in the hospital, everybody watches you all the time. Every little thing you do, somebody notices. It's hard to explain, but when I was there, the whole world was about me."

"Tough to get over, isn't it, Rell?"

I was beginning to wonder if it were worth it.

"Don't say another word." Emi's back stiffened.

"Emi, listen."

"Don't talk. Wanda's coming down the hall."

"Re-el." Wanda's voice sounded like a cat in heat. "Look at you!" She ran her hand over my scalp. She touched my head.

My shoulders tensed. My face flushed. I wanted to pounce on her, and tear out her tongue. *I am not public property. You cannot go around touching my head.*

"You are a courageous soul." Wanda was purring.

Emi grabbed my arm. "Rell, come on, we're late," she said. "We have to go."

"What's the rush?" Wanda asked.

"We have an appointment with Mr. Owens. He's starting a peer sensitivity group." Emi dragged me down the hall. "We should be there already."

"What's the group about?" Wanda asked.

"How not to be an asshole. Want to come?" Emi asked.

The two of us sprinted down the hall and around the corner. "Safe," Emi said.

"Until next time."

"How'd you like the sensitivity group idea?" Emi smiled.

"Brilliant."

Emi crossed her eyes and stuck out her tongue. "Wanda Ya-manaka, poster girl for the sensitivity impaired."

The first period bell rang.

"Emi, I'm sorry," I said. "For everything."

"Me too," Emi said. "I don't want to fight anymore."

Emi stroked the top of my head with her hand. "Jack Flynn is right. You do have guts."

"A friend of mine told me I was wearing my wig like it was a merit badge."

"Your friend should think before she says things."

"I think she was right," I said. "But, just in case." I opened my backpack and showed her my Hat-Hair wig. "I've got the situation covered."

Emi hugged me. The corner of her books hit my scar.

"Do you remember the last time we fought like that?" she asked.

I shook my head.

"It was when we were thirteen, and you told Sara that I was afraid I was a boy because I didn't get my period yet."

I covered my face. "I forgot about that."

"It was a low blow," Emi said. "But Sara was cool with it."

Then I got scared. "I can't do this," I told Emi. "I'm putting the wig on."

"Stop it, Rell. Most of the kids already saw you in the hall way."

"I know, but...."

"Fine," Emi said. "I'll get Wanda to meet you in the girls' room so she can help you on with it. It would make such a great story for the school paper." Emi waved her finger in the air, pretending to read a newspaper headline. "Rell Puts Wig Back On."

A surge of anti-Wanda shot through me. "You know what buttons to push, don't you?"

"That's what friends are for." She grinned.

"I wish you could come to English with me," I said.

"Go!"

When I walked into English class, all I got were a few smiles—nothing out of the ordinary.

It was harder in the cafeteria at lunch. Kids did stare and whisper, and there were the double takes and jabbing friends, but it wasn't anything I couldn't handle.

I looked around for Nate, but he wasn't around. He didn't call me on Sunday, but between Emi, LB, the mall, and everything else that went on, I hadn't realized it.

All through lunch I looked for him. I replayed our Saturday night date.

Maybe he was sick of me, I thought. Maybe I shouldn't have taken off my wig at the beach. It was the wig, I thought. It was too much for him to handle. It was the wig or the no sex.

By the middle of lunch, I was convinced we were broken up.

"You think too much," Emi said.

"It was more than the wig," I said. "We had a fight. Well, not a fight, but I don't know, it wasn't good."

"What did you fight about?"

"Nothing," I said. "But I think we broke up."

It had to be the no sex, I thought.

"Maybe it's for the best," Emi said.

"Maybe he's sick."

"Or maybe his grandfather's dying of cancer again." As soon as she said it, she stiffened. "Oh, Rell, I'm sorry. I didn't mean to say that."

"It's okay, Emi."

"That was an awful thing to say."

"It would have been hilarious at Stanhope," I said.

"Maybe he *is* sick," Emi said. "But nothing serious," she quickly added.

"His truck may have broken down on the way to school," I said. "Last weekend it took three tries before it would start."

"Could be."

"Besides, he'd never dump me like that. He's too nice a guy."

"Not everybody thinks so," Emi said.

"Like who?"

"Never mind."

"Who?"

"Kalani," she said. "He said Nate has a bad temper."

"How does your brother know him?"

"Nate beat up one of his friends for no reason. They were playing basketball, and his friend blocked Nate's shot, and Nate cold-cocked him."

"Nate Lee? Geek? Honor Society President?"

"Kalani said Nate kept coming back every night picking fights with guys on the court."

"Why didn't you tell me this before?" I asked.

"I didn't think you'd believe me."

"Maybe it was somebody else," I said.

"No, it was Nate," Emi insisted. "He's not as nice as you think, Rell."

Kalani had to be wrong.

That afternoon after school, I sat on my bed with a bowl of Rocky Road ice cream on my lap. I stared at my phone, willing it to ring. I picked up my history book and read the same paragraph four times over before I gave up. At four-thirty, I couldn't stand it anymore, and I called Nate.

"Where were you today?" I asked.

"Whoa!" Nate said. "Can you start out with a hello?"

"I was worried about you," I said.

"I have a mother for that, thank you."

"I went to school today. Bald."

"You're not bald, Rell."

"Where *were* you?"

"I had something to take care of," Nate said.

"Is that the best answer I get?"

"Lucky you got that," he aid.

"I needed you."

Why did I say that? Wrong. Wrong. Wrong.

"I needed to talk to you." I got it out as fast as I could. "Well, I needed to talk to you last night." I was blubbering.

"So talk."

"Never mind," I said. Then I asked, "Nate, did you ever play basketball in Lanikai?"

"You needed to know if I played basketball in Lanikai?"

"No. I was just wondering," I said. "Emi's brother, Kalani, said he knew you."

"I used to," he said. "Now I play at the courts behind the police station."

The police station. "Why there?"

"If you must know, it's because you don't have to pay for the lights at that court."

"Well, that's okay," I said.

"I'm glad you approve." His voice was cold.

"Sorry," I said. One more apology. "I missed you."

Oh God, I told him I missed him. Wrong move. Change topics.

"Cyril had a meltdown because I was late to class," I said. "She piled us with homework. What time are you coming over?"

"Rell, can you get through your homework yourself?" Nate asked.

"Why?"

"My parents don't ask me this many questions," he said.

"Sorry. I didn't mean it." I was sick of hearing myself apologize.

"It's no big deal," Nate said. "I'm going over to Paul Cruz's house to help him with his brother's twenty-first birthday party."

"I didn't know you hung out with Paul."

"There's a lot you don't know, Rell. I'll see you tomorrow."

"Wait."

"What now?"

"Have fun," I said.

"I will." He hung up.

"And, by the way, LB is dying, and you are an absolute asshole," I said it to the dial tone.

I got another bowl of ice cream and emailed LB.

I wish you were here with me, Rell, she wrote.

Me, too, I answered.

You were right about the Fred Hutch doctor. He wants me to try a new treatment.

At Stanhope or in Seattle?

Seattle.

When do you leave?

Right after they get this infection under control, she wrote. *I may have pneumonia.*

How are you otherwise, I wrote.

I've been getting nosebleeds a lot, and I'm getting platelets.

Nick had nosebleeds a lot before he died, and the last time I saw him, he was getting platelets. I kissed the top of his head and left a lipstick kiss on it. "It's to keep you loved," I told him.

Rell, if things don't go well, will you come to visit me? LB wrote.

Just say the word, Roomie.

The next night her email was worse. Her parents had arrived that morning, and later that day she had a seizure. The doctors said it was a reaction to her medications, "Not that uncommon," Doctor Lynch told her.

I shut down my computer and prayed, but not to some white-bearded God who let kids die. I prayed to all the kids who died from cancer. I knew they were watching; they knew what was happening, and I begged them not to let LB die.

"Please," I prayed.

I knew they wouldn't let me down.

Chapter Twelve

Within a few days, LB was doing better. Her infection was gone, and the nosebleeds had stopped. But sometimes I would get a mental flash of her dying. I could see her funeral—her parents, Doc Lynch. It was a replay of Tess's funeral, except I was sitting alone.

It was toughest at night. I had nightmares about her dying. One night I woke up and my mother was holding me. I had been crying in my sleep.

I needed to talk to Dr. Maitlin about what was happening. I was seeing LB and Tess in my dreams, I thought I saw the two of them walking down the hall in school. I was obsessed with LB dying.

When I went to my next appointment with Dr. Maitlin, the first thing she said was, "Wow! No wig."

I brushed the top of my head with my hand. "Yeah."

"You hair looks like it has some curl to it," she said.

"Maybe a little more curl than it did before."

"How did it go at school without the wig?"

"A couple of kids stared."

"Anything else?"

"When I was in the girls' room, I watched a girl walk behind me and sneak a look in the mirror at me. But most kids were okay.

So, I guess I'm a regular kid again, except for LB." I wanted to get to the point.

"What's happening with her?" Dr. Maitlin asked.

"Lots of stuff." My tears were already fighting to get out. "She's dying."

Dr. Maitlin leaned forward. "Tell me about it," she said.

I nodded.

"How do you feel?"

"Sad."

"What else?"

"Scared."

"Scared. How?"

"I don't know." I shrugged.

"Try to explain."

"I don't know," I said. "It's like I'm Cinderella and it's right before midnight." I looked up at her. "Do you know what I mean?"

"I think so."

"Do you think I'm crazy?"

"No." She smiled. "Not at all." She leaned forward more, resting her elbows on her knees.

I looked down at my hands. On the way over, in the car, I ate an orange. My fingernails had some of the white pith under them. It looked like I had a French manicure.

"Rell, what happens when the clock strikes midnight?"

"I die," I said.

Dr. Maitlin didn't say anything at first, then, in a soft, calm voice, she said, "It's natural for you to be afraid, Rell. Your best friend is dying from the same disease you had."

"No," I shouted. "She has leukemia. ANL."

"But you both had cancer."

Mine was different. I had Hodgkin's disease. It's a good cancer if you have to have one.

"Rell, for a while, anyone's illness, even a movie star's, or someone very old person's, may trigger a fear of death for you. With LB, she's very close to you, and it's much harder."

I didn't say anything.

"And sometimes, when someone we know relapses, or doesn't respond to treatment, we experience a feeling of relief. Something like being happy that it's them and not us."

"You think I'm happy that LB is dying?"

"That's not what I'm saying. It's like when a teacher asks a question that you don't know the answer to. When she calls on someone else, you're happy it wasn't you." She paused. "I'm saying that when someone relapses, there is a natural feeling that the odds of surviving cancer just got better for you. Like death has a quota, and you've been spared. Even if the person who is dying is a good friend, there's a natural survival instinct we all have that makes us relieved that it's not us who is dying."

"How can you say that?"

Dr. Maitlin sat up. "Rell, you should be aware that LB's condition may also trigger some symptoms in you. You may experience phantom pain. Night sweats. Loss of appetite. Have you had any unusual symptoms?"

"No." I shook my head. It wasn't really a lie, well, only a little one.

In the shower that morning, I felt the slightest pea-sized knot in my neck. But when I fluttered my fingers over it, I decided it was a vein.

"No. Nothing." Tears were dripping off my chin.

"What's the matter, Rell?"

"Everything."

Dr. Maitlin held my hands in hers, gently, like she was holding an injured bird, and then she said, "It's all part of the healing process."

I smelled her perfume, and felt the warmth of her breath.

"Everything is coming apart," I said.

The next morning before school, I watched Ajax twist and turn and scratch his back against the grass in the yard. His biggest concerns in life were stray cats and the occasional flea. Wouldn't it be great to go through life as a dog? Just rolling around in the dirt all day. No parents. No worries and no school.

That day in English class Mr. Meyers returned our poems. He wrote on mine, "Your work shows extreme maturity and depth of feeling. Would you mind sharing it with the class?"

Yes, I would mind. I told him I didn't want to, and he said that was okay.

During History class, Frank Acoba pivoted his notebook toward Paul Cruz. Frank had drawn a naked butt. Under it he wrote, "No one listens to you until you fart."

I smiled.

Mr. Fields smiled back at me.

I'm not smiling at you. Why would I smile at you? Because you gave me such a terrific welcome my first day back at school? I don't think so. What about your blockbuster lectures? No, that's not it either.

Paul Cruz flashed his sketch of a naked woman on a motorcycle to Frank. When I saw it, my first thought was that he drew the woman without any scars. Everyone I knew at Stanhope had at least one.

At lunchtime, I had lunch with Emi.

"Rell, are you with me?" Emi's voice sounded far away.

I wanted her to leave me alone. I wanted to keep floating—I was at Stanhope, watching LB sleep in her bed.

"Rell, do you want to go?" Emi shoved an invitation in my ace.

"A Garden Show of Prom Gowns" at Neiman Marcus. "It's free," she said.

Mary, Mary, quite contrary. How does your garden grow?

The invitation had a border of sunflowers and daisies with orange butterflies fluttering through a vine.

With dreams of hell and cancer cells, that's how my garden grows.

"It might be fun," Emi said.

My garden is full of weeds.

"Rell?"

I kept floating.

"Rell." Emi grabbed my shoulders. "Rell!"

The next thing I knew I was in the school nurse's room. The dragon was scratching at the window. He wanted to come in.

"Rell." It was my mother's voice.

"Come on, stand up, Sweetheart," she said.

Then Dad was there, and I was in his car. "You're going to be okay, Rell," he said.

"Rell." I heard Dr. Maitlin's voice. I was out of the car, in a room, floating. "Do you know who I am?" she asked.

Of course, I know who you are. Where's LB?

"Rell, answer me," Dr. Maitlin said. "Do you know where you are?"

I looked around. Doctors. Nurses. Metal Beds. I'm in a hospital. She should know that.

"Rell, I'm Dr. Yim." It was a new voice. "You're going to feel a small sting," the doctor said.

I'm falling down a hole.

He gave me a needle.

"Rell?" the doctor called me.

I'm right here. Can't you see me?

I heard him say, "This should keep her calm."

I'm falling.

I saw Dad standing at the foot of my bed. He had his arm around Mom.

Catch me, Dad. But he didn't, and I kept on falling.

When I woke up, Dr. Maitlin was sitting next to my bed, reading. "How are you doing, Rell?" She closed her book.

I looked around the room. Dr. Maitlin was the only person there.

"Your parents went to get some breakfast. I'll get them if you'd like."

I didn't answer.

"Rell, I'm going to call the nurse to stay with you while I go to the cafeteria."

"No." My voice sounded like an echo. "Stay."

She nodded.

I closed my eyes, and as soon as I did, the falling started again. It was as if I were drifting down, through the mattress, through the floor, down into somewhere I couldn't describe.

"Stay," I said.

"Sure," she said. "I'll page them."

I stared at the ceiling as she made her call. The ceiling tiles around the air-conditioning vent were gray from dust.

When Dr. Maitlin got off the phone she said, "Do you know what happened yesterday?"

Yesterday. I had lost a day.

"You passed out in the cafeteria," she said.

I remembered the dragon scratching at the window in the nurse's room, but that was it. So I passed out. "Were there many kids around?" I asked.

"Emi was with you. And another friend who got the school nurse."

"How did I get to the health room?"

"By the time the nurse got to you, you had already come to and you walked to her office. No one saw more than that."

Everybody saw me.

I turned my face away from her, pushing my cheek into the pillow. The pillowcase was stenciled with black letters: Honolulu General Hospital.

"Was anybody else there?" I asked.

"I don't know."

I wondered if Nate was there.

I curled myself around my pillow, keeping my back to Dr. Maitlin. "Was I crying?"

"No one mentioned that," she said. "Why would you think that you were crying?"

Because of LB.

Dr. Maitlin rubbed my back, light, in small circles, like my mother used to do when I was young.

"The last thing I remember was looking down at LB. It was like I was a camera mounted on the ceiling of her room, then I zoomed in closer and closer. LB was dying. Then the camera zoomed in right to her face. And it wasn't LB's face. It was me."

"It's okay," Dr. Maitlin said, and then the door to my room swung open.

A doctor I had never met walked in, followed by my parents. Mom and Dad looked scared. I had seen that look before, when I first got diagnosed. They were terrified.

I needed them not to be afraid. Parents aren't supposed to be afraid. Parents are supposed to fix things and make them better.

The doctor introduced himself. "I'm Dr. Yim, Chief of Psychiatric Services." As he spoke, he read over my chart, made a few notes. "You gave us quite a scare, young lady."

He made it sound like I did it on purpose.

"Are you going to follow up, Jeanne?" He asked Dr. Maitlin.

She nodded.

"Family sessions?" Dr. Yim asked.

"Starting this week," she answered.

"All of us?" I asked Dr. Maitlin.

"Yes."

I had told her so many things I didn't want my parents to know.

"Mr. and Mrs. DeMello, may I see you in the hall?" Dr. Yim asked.

Mom and Dad exchanged glances.

"We'll be right outside the door," Dad said to me.

Mom kissed my cheek and ran her hand over my face. Her eyes were red, her mouth drawn, and she smelled like cigarettes. "I love you, Sweetheart," she said.

"If you need us, just whistle," Dad said and winked.

I smiled.

"We love you, Rell," he said.

"I know."

When they left, I asked Dr. Maitlin, "When we're all together, you won't tell them anything I said to you, will you?"

"I can't, Rell."

"But will you?"

"I'd never do that, Rell."

I wasn't sure. "They fight all the time," I said.

"You told me."

"And now…I just made it worse."

"Rell, we're all concerned," she said, "but the focus is on you, not us."

Yeah, the focus is on me. Emi would love to hear that, I thought.

"I have to go now," she said. "We'll see each other in a few days, but if you need to call me, you know the number."

I nodded.

"Take care, Rell."

When she left the room, I sneaked a look at my chart. Dr. Maitlin had written, "Possible post-traumatic stress episode. Suggest intensive therapy and family sessions."

Dr. Yim had written, "Normal adolescent reaction."

Normal? I couldn't find normal if I had a life-sized map.

I wasn't released from the hospital until almost four o'clock. There were paperwork problems in the hospital. There were always paperwork problems.

On the drive home, Dad went through a yellow light. Mom looked over at him, but she didn't say anything. He kept his eyes straight ahead. Both of them chatted with me about the local news, and the weather, as if I were a houseguest who just flew in from the moon. They talked to each other about the gas bill, the weeds in the yard, and a possible trip to the Big Island for summer vacation. They talked about everything and anything but what just happened.

I wanted to tell them to stop, that it was okay. I knew I passed out. I knew I was crazy, and I just announced it to everyone in the school cafeteria.

We pulled into the driveway. Dad opened the car door for me and Mom held my elbow as if I were some ninety-year-old cripple.

She got me settled in my room. "I washed your sheets," she said. She plumped up my pillows. She brought in dinner on a tray. It was the breakfast tray that Dad and I bought her for Mother's Day one year. Then she told me to get some rest, but it was hard to rest. The two of them were fighting. I heard Mom ask Dad why he couldn't commute from Hilo. "It's a forty-five-minute plane ride," she said.

"You know what the beginning of a job is like," Dad said. "I don't work a forty-hour week, Maria."

"I can't handle this myself," Mom said.

The "this" they were talking about was me.

"What do you want me to do? Quit my job and stay home and watch you wallow in your depression?"

"That's not fair, David," she said.

"Life's not fair, Maria, or didn't you notice that."

"At least I face up to what's going on around here. You just hide."

There was a slam of a fist on a table.

"You use work to hide," Mom said. "Run away, David. It's what you do best."

"I work my ass off, just to pay the bills," Dad said. "You don't contribute a damn thing," Dad said. "Chinese herbs. Cancer books and that damn psychologist. Now we all have to see her. She'll be able to buy a car for what's she's going to charge."

"We need to talk to her, David."

"I don't need to pay to hear you whine. I get enough of that for free."

Please stop fighting.

I folded my pillow around my head to block out their voices.

"Damnit, David. You need to see her more than the rest of us."

"What I need is a wife who can handle things."

"The Great David DeMello! He doesn't need to talk to anyone. He can take care of everything himself!" Mom was screaming. "There's nothing the Great David DeMello can't do!"

"I'm the only one in this family who is not falling apart."

Daddy, do you think I'm falling apart?

"Don't ever say that, David! Don't even think it."

I stopped listening.

I flew away—down the steps of an oak-stained staircase. I held on to the rail and lifted my feet and I flew. The staircase switched back twice, down to landings with Chinese carpets on them and velvet chairs at the bottom. And I flew away until morning.

When I woke up the next morning, a huge bouquet of birds of paradise, orchids, *pikake,* and ginger was on the kitchen counter.

I thought the flowers were from Nate. I read the card, "To my most beautiful star. I love you, Dad."

Nothing but the best for his Estrella.

CHAPTER THIRTEEN

Mom was at the breakfast table, reading the paper. She had her cell pone right next to her coffee mug.

"Morning, Mom."

She kissed me. I smelled cigarettes on her.

"What can I make you for breakfast?" she asked.

"I can do it." I took a bowl out of the cupboard. "Cereal's fine."

"How are you feeling?" she asked.

"Fine."

"Emi called you," she said. "You may want to give her a call." She sounded like she was trying to make normal morning conversation.

"I will."

"And Nate called several times."

I didn't feel like talking to anyone. I knew they'd ask questions. And Nate? Nice of him to phone in his concern.

"What are you doing today?" I asked.

"There's a sale on at Marsh's," Mom said. "Jeans are half-price." She opened the paper to show me the ad. She had highlighted what she was interested in with yellow marker. My mother couldn't read the paper without marking it up. There were notes in the margin, as if it were one of her students' papers. "And we have a family appointment with Dr. Maitlin at eleven," she said.

"Is Dad going?"

"He can't make it. Work," she said.

He doesn't want to make it work.

"Do you think he'll ever go?"

Mom put the paper down. "I'm not sure," she said. "He might, if you asked him."

"I don't think so," I said. I didn't think anything would get him to go.

I sat down next to my mother. "I want to ask you something, Mom."

"Shoot."

"Listen to the whole thing, before you say anything," I said.

"Okay."

"LB's not doing well, and I want to go to Stanhope to see her."

"Sure." She didn't even flinch.

There was something wrong. She gave in too easily.

"I'll call Dr. Kosaki right now. I'm sure he'll give me time off."

"No," I said. "I want to go by myself."

"It's a long trip," she said.

"It's not like I could get lost, Mom. The plane doesn't stop off in the middle of the ocean."

"You know what I mean, Rell."

"You could watch me board the plane at the airport, and LB's parents could pick me up. It would just be for a few days. Please."

"I'll have to talk to your father," she said.

"You know he'll leave it up to you," I said. "Can I go?"

"When do you want to leave?"

"Tomorrow?"

"I'll call Dad," she said. "Let's see what he can do. But tomorrow? Everything's probably booked."

Within an hour, Dad had arranged for my plane tickets, booked a limousine service to take me from the San Francisco Airport to

Stanhope, and reserved a room for me at Stanhope's Hospitality House. Making things happen is what Dad did best.

By the time it was all arranged, it was time to drive to Dr. Maitlin's.

On the way over, my mother asked three times if I was sure I wanted to go by myself. "It would be no problem for me to take off work," she insisted. "Are you sure you want to go by yourself?"

"I'm sure, Mom."

"How are LB's parents doing?" she asked.

"I guess they're okay."

Mom kept her eyes on the road when she asked me, "How bad is LB?"

"I think she's dying."

About a block away from Dr. Maitlin's office, Mom pulled into Starbuck's for a cappuccino. She almost made us late. She sat there in Dr. Maitlin's waiting room, sipping her drink. The whole office smelled like coffee.

Dr. Maitlin came out of her office. "Glad to see you both," she said.

Mom smiled.

"Come on in." She gestured for mom and me to go in her office.

I sat in my regular chair. Mom sat in the wooden rocker. She had her back to the shelves of dinosaurs and monsters. She sat up straight, with her feet flat on the floor. She had dark, puffy circles under her eyes.

Dr. Maitlin thanked Mom for coming, and sat in her regular chair—a slinky black leather chair with wide arms. She checked her watch. "Shall we give Mr. DeMello a few more minutes before we begin?"

I knew it was her way of asking if Dad was going to show up.

"He won't be coming," Mom said. "He wanted to be here, but he's on the Big Island. He was called in for an emergency.

Even Mom lies.

"He works long hours, doesn't he?" Dr. Maitlin asked.

"Yes. He's a project engineer," Mom said.

"Well, then, let's get started," Dr. Maitlin said and she went over the rules about privacy. She made it clear to Mom that she would not divulge anything that I told her in a session, unless I said it was okay. Then she looked over at me. "You understand that, right, Rell?"

I nodded.

"And you, Mrs. DeMello, do you understand?"

Mom said she did.

Dr. Maitlin paused, as if she were letting each of us catch our breath before we started. Then she asked me, "Rell, do you know what happened to you at school the other day?"

"Not really."

"What do you think happened?"

"I guess I passed out." I could see a reflection of myself in Dr. Maitlin's eyeglasses. I looked small and distorted.

"Do you remember any particular feeling or any thoughts you were having earlier that day?"

I didn't answer.

"Rell?" Dr. Maitlin was pushing for an answer.

"I felt like I was falling down a hole," I said. I didn't like talking like that in front of my mother. I knew it would make her upset.

"Could you see where the hole was?" Dr. Maitlin asked.

Out of the corner of my eye, I could seem my mother sitting absolutely motionless, as if she were hanging on my every word.

"It was in Alice's garden," I said. "But the Mad Hatter wasn't there. He was, but he was in Peter Rabbit's garden, too." It sounded so dumb when I said it.

"What happened when you fell down the hole, Rell?" Dr. Maitlin asked.

"Nothing. I just kept falling."

"Did anything happen just before that? Did something upset you? Or scare you?" Dr. Maitlin asked.

I was sure she was trying to get me to tell my mother about how I saw myself dying in LB's bed, but I wasn't going to do it.

"No, nothing," I answered.

"Nothing frightened or upset you?"

"No," I said. "Nothing. If something did happen, I would have told you already."

With that answer, she picked up that I wasn't going to say anything about it in front of my mother.

Dr. Maitlin switched gears. "How about you, Mrs. DeMello? How are things going at home?"

"It's a little tense," Mom said.

"In what way?"

"There's tension between me and Rell," she answered.

What about the tension between Dad and you?

"Can you be specific?" Dr. Maitlin asked her.

"Rell doesn't know how to take care of herself," Mom said. "She forgets to take her antibiotics. She doesn't eat right. And she never uses sunscreen."

"That's not true," I said.

"You don't take your vitamins, Rell," Mom said.

"They're not vitamins," I told Dr. Maitlin. "They're some Chinese herbs that she bought, and she doesn't even know what's in them."

"They are vitamins prescribed by a naturopath." Mom turned to Dr. Maitlin. "You see, everything is a battle when it comes to her health. She doesn't take care of herself."

"I do take care of myself!"

Dr. Maitlin waited until Mom and I calmed down then she said to me, "Sometimes after a child or a teenager has had a life-threatening illness, parents react by becoming overly vigilant." Then she turned to Mom. "As parents, we worry. We may become more strict. We want to control our child's life and protect her from everything and anything we can. The rules in the house may get tighter, or the punishment for breaking rules may become more harsh. This is all very common."

Mom nodded.

"Under normal circumstances, it's hard enough for a parent to figure out where to draw the boundaries for her child." The two of them smiled at each other as if they were members of the same secret-handshake mother club.

"But this is foreign territory for you, Mrs. DeMello," Dr. Maitlin said. "Right now you don't know where to draw that line or how much freedom to give Rell. There are no role models for you to look toward, and even if there were, it wouldn't matter," she said. "This is hard on both of you."

Dr. Maitlin continued, "Let's consider a different scenario. Mrs. DeMello, what do you think would happen if you let Rell do anything she wanted to?"

Mom took a sip of her coffee. She stared at a poster of tropical fish on the wall opposite of her. "She wouldn't take care of herself," she answered.

"I would, too, Mom."

Dr. Maitlin held up her hand, and I kept quiet.

"How would she not take care of herself?" Dr. Maitlin asked Mom.

Mom shook her head. I could see tears forming in her eyes. She didn't answer.

"What about it, Rell? Would you take care of yourself?" she asked me. "Would you take your medication?"

"Yes."

"Do you take them everyday?"

"Most days. But some days I forget…not many though."

"How about your eating habits? Do you eat well?"

"For God's sake, I eat!"

"Why does that question upset you, Rell?"

"Because my mother is crazy about me eating all the time. *Eat.* She keeps stuffing food down my throat like it's some kind of cure for cancer."

Dr. Maitlin addressed Mom. "Often with cancer patients, eating is a common source of tension between the patient and her family—whether the patient is the child, the spouse, or the parent. The caregiver wants to see the patient eat. It makes them feel better. It's a sign that things are back to normal. It's something they can do to make the cancer go away."

Mom dabbed the tears from her cheeks.

"Parents want to nurture their children. It's what we're programmed to do—birds, lions, men and women—we want to feed them," she said. "But teenagers want to be independent. They want be like all their friends. So the battle often boils down to the Mom screaming 'Eat' and the teen screaming 'I don't want to eat.'"

"It's more than food," Mom said. "She does the opposite of whatever I ask her to do. Sometimes it's to the point of her being irresponsible."

"Give me an example of how you're irresponsible, Rell."

"She doesn't—" Mom started to answer.

"I've asked Rell, Mrs. DeMello," Dr. Maitlin interrupted Mom.

"I am responsible," I said. "I go to school. I get good grades." I looked over at my mother. "Girls my age get pregnant. I know lots of kids who are drunk out of their minds every day at school. I *am* responsible, Mom."

"What else, Rell?" Dr. Maitlin asked.

"What more is there? I don't do drugs, except for chemo, and my only tattoos are from radiation."

"You're not careful, Rell," Mom said. "How many times have you forgotten to take your antibiotics?"

"Missing a few pills isn't going to kill me, Mom."

"What if you get an infection?"

"I know what an infection feels like."

"You're supposed to take your meds everyday," Mom said.

"I do!"

"You don't. You just said so."

"You don't care about me. You just want to catch me in a lie!"

"I want to keep you alive, Rell."

"By standing over me twenty-four hours a day?"

"If I have to."

"You can't keep me alive, Mom!"

"I can!"

"Tell her!" I screamed at Dr. Maitlin. "Nobody can keep me alive. The cancer can come back anytime it wants to. Nothing can stop it. Not her, not Dr. Braden, not me. Nobody." The tears poured out of me. "Cancer doesn't care. Tell her."

It was like a bomb went off, and the dust had to settle, and the cloud had to lift before we could tally up the score and see who won, who lost, and who was wounded worse.

"My mom thinks she has a magic wand," I told Dr. Maitlin. "Like she can keep my cancer away. She should know better.

"Talk to your mother, Rell, not me," Dr. Maitlin said. "Explain how you feel to her."

I stared down at my lap. "Sometimes I think you don't see me," I said. "You just see cancer. You stare at my neck where the cancer was." I looked at my mother. "How would you like it if I stared at your chest all the time and asked you if you had breast cancer yet? Your mom had it, and she died." I felt my heart pounding.

"That's different, Rell."

"No it isn't."

"I've never had cancer," Mom said.

"How do you know you don't have it right now?"

God, why did I say that?

"I'm sorry, Rell."

"And stop being sorry all the time!"

Another quiet.

I looked to Dr. Maitlin. "Tell her she can't keep the cancer away."

"Mrs. DeMello, do you believe you can control Rell's cancer?"

"I know I can't control some of the risk factors," she answered. "However, I can make her more aware of her condition." Mom ran her fingers through her hair. "I can make sure she takes her medications and gets plenty of rest. And, yes, I can make sure she eats well. God forbid I would want my daughter to eat well."

"I'll ask you again, Mrs. DeMello. Do you think you can control your daughter's cancer?"

Mom sighed. "When Rell first got sick I should have been more aware. I should have noticed changes in her. If I did, maybe things would have been different."

"Rell had no symptoms other than the lump. Is that right?"

Mom nodded.

"So, there were no changes to be aware of, until the lump appeared," Dr. Maitlin said.

As the two of them talked, I studied the swirl on the carpet, from my chair, to Dr. Maitlin's chair, to Mom's.

"Mrs. DeMello, what do you mean things would have been different?"

"I should have insisted on more tests. It took the doctors five months to diagnose her. I should have forced them to look for things faster. Maybe she would have only been a Stage I cancer and wouldn't have had to do both chemo and radiation."

"Do you think it was your fault that Rell was diagnosed late?"

"Maybe."

Dr. Maitlin took off her glasses. "The sad truth is that we all treat doctors as if they were gods. And, as gods, they are supposed to be infallible. So when they are wrong, our trust in the entire medical system erodes. We're like children who find out that their parents aren't perfect."

"But maybe things would have been different if I pushed," Mom said.

"There's no way to know that," Dr. Maitlin said. "Mrs. DeMello, I'd like a yes or no answer to my question. Do you think you can control Rell's cancer?"

"Deep down, yes," Mom said.

I knew it.

"Okay, let's move on." Dr. Maitlin looked at me, then she looked at Mom. "Each of you loves the other very much." She settled her eyes on me. "You both know that."

I gave a slight nod.

"What you have to do now is to learn how to trust each other in ways that you never had to before. This is all new for you. Rell, that means that your mother has to know with deep certainty that you are not putting your health at risk. She has to know that you will tell her if something—anything—is bothering you. She's your mother. She has a right to know that. And you, Mrs. DeMello, you have to begin to let go and allow Rell take responsibility for herself."

"But—" Mom interrupted.

"Please let me finish," Dr. Maitlin said. "Rell told me she wants to go away to college."

"How can I let her go away when—" Mom interrupted again.

"Please, Mrs. DeMello."

Mom sat back.

"First of all, that issue is years away. But the question you should be asking isn't 'How can I allow her to go away?' but rather 'How can I prepare her to live independently?' That means giving her the opportunity to make her own choices and trusting that she will do the right thing in the long run. Of course she'll make mistakes on the way. It's part of learning and growing up. It's how we all learn—one issue at a time."

Mom nodded.

"I have an assignment for both of you," Dr. Maitlin said. "For the next few days I want you both to pretend that Rell is on vacation from cancer. Mrs. DeMello, I want you to pretend that Rell is not at risk for anything, not even a common cold. When you feel yourself wanting to protect her, you say to yourself, 'Just for today, cancer is not going to get Rell.' Is that a deal?"

We both agreed.

"There will be no discussion of cancer unless Rell brings it up." She looked at Mom. "It also means that if Rell does something wrong, she should be punished for it. Right now marks the end of any special treatment for her. There will be no special food, no special curfew, no decisions made based on her medical history."

Then she looked at me. "That also means you can't ask for special privileges. There's no getting out of chores or bids for sympathy from anyone. Got it?"

"Uh-huh."

"And remember, Rell, you have to be honest with your mother. If you have any concerns or questions about your health, you *must* talk to her about it."

"Okay."

On the ride home Mom and I didn't look at each other. We didn't speak to each other. It was if we had seen each other naked in the locker room and we were too embarrassed to face each other.

CHAPTER FOURTEEN

Before I went to bed that night, I checked my neck in the mirror. That pea-shaped lump was still there. I took out a pen and rolled it over the node, just like Dr. Braden taught me to do. Then I measured the line. It was less than one-eighth inch long.

"Cancer feels like a hard pea," Dr. Braden said. "It doesn't roll or move."

I tried to roll the node. It wouldn't move. I squeezed it between my fingers and tried to shove it around, but it didn't move.

I told myself it couldn't be back, but I new it could. One minute I was sure I was fine. Cancer was over. The next I was sure I relapsed. I sat on my bed and slid my hand over the node again, then I buried my face in my pillow and cried. At first it was just a whimper, then a muffled sob. Then it was full-blown crying loud enough for my mother to hear me in the kitchen.

Maybe I wanted her to hear me.

She came in, sat next to me, and wrapped her arms around me.

"It's not fair," I said. "It's not fair."

"You're right, Rell. It's not fair." She held me.

"I hate cancer," I said.

"Maybe LB's just hitting a bad time," Mom said.

She thought I was crying about LB.

"Sometimes I'm afraid," I said.

"Don't give up hope yet."

"Sometimes I'm afraid it could happen to me," I said it like I was fishing, throwing a line out to my mother to see what I'd get back.

"It's like Dr. Maitlin said, Rell. Everything is so fresh for you. In a few years, when there aren't so many follow-up tests, it'll be easier."

She didn't have a clue.

"My tests were good last time, right?" I needed to hear it one more time.

"They were perfect."

The cancer couldn't have grown back in a week. I knew that. That pea must be a swollen gland, or an overgrown zit.

"Rell, once you go back to school, and get back into sports and debate, you'll begin to feel like you never left."

"I don't want to go back to school," I said.

"You don't have to go back until after you come back from seeing LB."

"I don't ever want to go back."

"Rell...."

"I want to transfer," I said. "Why can't I go to Oahu School for Girls? Dad always wanted me to go to a girls' school."

"Rell, now's not the time to be talking about this."

"Please, Mom. I can never go back to Kailua."

"This is a big decision. All three of us need to talk about this," she said. "In fact, it may be something we should discuss with Dr. Maitlin."

"We don't to talk to her about *everything*," I said.

"She could help put it in perspective for us," Mom said.

"How would you like to face all those kids after you what happened?"

"Rell, you're a strong young woman," Mom said. "You're stronger than you think."

I'm sick of being strong.

"I wish my mother were alive to see you. She'd be so proud of you."

I could hardly remember my Grandmom Toni; she died when I was five years old.

"She was an elegant lady, Rell—just like you." Mom's eyes welled up. "And the way you've handled being sick…I'm not sure I could have handled it as well. You come from good stock," she said. "Strong Portuguese women."

"Yeah," I said. "Cabral and DeMello women. They had their babies in the fields and went right back to work," I joked.

"And before they went to bed at night they baked bread," Mom said.

"And chopped wood for the fire," I added.

"And do you know what the Cabral and DeMello women are most famous for?" she asked me.

I shook my head.

"Making their daughters hearty suppers."

I held up my watch. "Mom, you couldn't go three hours without trying to feed me."

"Not true," she said. "This is normal conversation for any Portuguese woman."

"Okay, I'll give you that."

It was true. Portuguese women had to feed everyone, all the time. It was who Mom was. Before cancer, during treatment, and now.

"Rell," Mom said, "did you call Emi back yet?"

I shook my head.

"How about Nate?"

"Not yet." I wanted Nate to go away.

"Just give them a quick call," she said. "They're concerned about you."

"Okay," I said, but I didn't. I was too busy searching cancer websites for symptoms of relapse of Hodgkin's disease.

I soaped my neck and slithered my fingers over the node at least ten times. It was smaller, I was sure of it.

Life was good—but not for LB. She emailed me that her tests confirmed that she had pneumonia.

It would be easier on my parents if I died, she wrote.

LB's parents both worked in a computer assembly plant. Her father worked a lot of double shifts to help pay the bills. A few times the plant had a bake sale for her family, to help them with money.

My mother is still here, LB wrote.

Don't even think about dying, I answered.

It would be easier all around, she wrote.

No, it wouldn't be, I wrote. *What if your brother was sick? Would you think it would be better if he died?*

That's a dumb question, LB wrote.

Because you know I'm right.

I'm tired, Rell, she wrote.

She was writing that more and more often.

Talk to me just a little more, I wrote.

I can't, she answered. *I'm going to bed.*

I love you, LB, I wrote.

Right back at you, Roomie.

Mom was on the phone when I walked in the kitchen. "Yes, Dr. Kosaki," she exaggerated his name as she spoke to let me know it was her boss on the phone. "She's much better. Thank you for asking." Mom cradled the phone between her ear and her shoulder and pulled out a pan of leftover lasagna from the refrigerator. Ajax sat right next to her, begging.

"Yes," she said. "I'm sure I'll be back on Monday." She laid the lasagna on the counter. "Absolutely," she said. "Don't change any of my appointments. I'll be there." There was a pause. "Thank you. I'll see you then."

"Does the whole world know about what happened?" I asked her.

"When the school nurse called, I was in a department meeting," Mom said. "So she called the department secretary to leave a message. All Dr. Kosaki knows is that you got sick." She got lettuce out of the fridge. "Do you want tomatoes and olives on your salad?"

"No salad," I said.

"Set the table for me, will you, honey. Just two plates."

That meant that Dad wouldn't be home to eat with us.

"Did you call Emi and Nate back yet?" she asked.

Why was she so obsessed with me calling them back?

"Faye and Sharlene called you, too," she said. "Why don't you call now?"

It was the only way I could get my mother off my back, so I called Emi. The first thing she asked was, "Are you okay?"

"Yeah."

"What happened?" she said.

"I thought you could tell me," I said. "I don't remember a thing."

"I was talking to you about the prom show. Remember?"

"Uh-huh. At Nieman's."

"And your eyes rolled up way up in your head, and you passed out on the table."

"You mean *on* the table? Into my food?"

"No. You knocked over my soda, but you missed everything else," she said. "Then Faye ran for the school nurse, and Nate and I stayed with you. By the time the nurse got to the cafeteria you already came to and walked to her office."

"Nate was there?"

"He kept the kids away from you."

"Was there a crowd around me?"

"No, not really. Well, maybe for a minute or two. But after you came to, nobody paid attention."

"Did they send an ambulance for me?"

"No, Miss High Drama. Your parents picked you up."

"That's right," I said. "I remember."

"An before you ask, you walked into the car—no stretcher."

"But everyone saw me pass out."

"Rell, the whole thing took five minutes. Most kids probably thought you were drunk."

"That makes me feel oh so much better."

"Rell, it wasn't as bad as you think."

"And Abe Lincoln never told a lie."

"That was George Washington who never lied," Emi corrected me.

"I'm never going back to Kailua," I said.

"Don't flatter yourself, Rell. By Monday you'll be old news."

"I won't be there on Monday. I'm going to San Francisco to see LB. She's dying." I wanted to get that out right in front.

"Sorry," she said.

"Me too."

"Have you told Nate you're going?"

I just told her LB was dying, and all she could ask me was if I called Nate. Emi was never going to understand.

"I haven't talked to him," I said.

"He calls your house a lot," Emi said. "You know, Rell, he's a really nice guy, and he likes you—big time."

"Since when did you become such a Nate Lee fan?"

"When you sit in a hospital waiting room with someone for seven hours, you run out of small talk. You get to know them fast."

"I didn't know Nate was at the hospital."

Why didn't my mother tell me that Emi and Nate were there?

"Nate drove me over there from school, and we stayed until your parents made us go home. I was wrong about him, Rell."

"What about the stuff your brother said about him?"

"My brother's a jerk. He probably made the whole thing up. You should call Nate," Emi said.

"I will."

"I'm going to hang up right now, so you can call him," Emi said.

"You call him for me," I told her.

"What?"

"Emi, please."

"Why?"

"I can't talk to him," I said. "I don't know if I can face him again."

"That's ridiculous."

"Please, Emi."

"This is beginning to reek of Sweet Valley High."

"If you don't call him, he'll never hear from me again. Please, Emi."

"Okay. Okay. What do you want me to say?"

"Can you ask him to come over tomorrow night, but not to call me or anything?"

"Anything else?"

"He can't ask me any questions about what happened."

"Any more rules?"

"No."

"You owe me for this," she said.

"I owe you big."

Friday morning I didn't get out of bed until nine o'clock. Mom was potting plants next to the barbecue pit.

I slid the patio glass door open. "I thought you had a student conference this morning," I said.

"My student cancelled on me." She put down the pot and wiped the sweat from her face with her forearm. She bent back from her waist, and rubbed the bottom of her spine. "It's tough getting old," she said.

Mom was wearing one of Dad's old T-shirts. "Come over here and talk to me," she said. "I need a break."

"I'll be right out."

I brought out a cup of coffee for mom, and orange juice for myself. I made it to mom's chair without spilling a drop, despite Ajax herding me.

Mom lifted a clay pot. "Slugs! They're chewing up my basil," she said.

"Mrs. Zoller said that if you put beer into a saucer and put it under the pot, the slugs will drown in it."

"I hate slugs." Mom angled the herb to the sun. The slimy slug trails shone in the sun. "Right after I finish up, I'm going to Safeway to get beer, and I'm going to pour it in every plant saucer I have. It'll be a Slug Happy Hour!"

Mom pointed to the next to the tree. "I dug out two buckets of mint this morning. It was taking over everything."

She took off her gardening gloves, exposing clean, pink hands at the end of dirt-veiled arms. "I was thinking of planting night-blooming jasmine under your window. That way you could smell it when you go to bed."

"Do you think Dr. Maitlin would think that was a special privilege?" I kidded.

"I think plants are within the rules."

"What do you think of her?" I asked Mom.

"She's certainly effective." Mom raised her eyebrows. "She brings up good points and she's fair. Look what happened yesterday."

"It was pretty intense," I said.

Mom and I sat on the chairs under the mango tree.

"Do you want to get some things out in the open now?" Mom asked. "No pressure. No questions. Just talk."

"Maybe another time," I said.

"What if I go first?" Mom put down her coffee mug. "Trust Building 101." She took in a deep breath. "Rell, you were right when you told Dr. Maitlin that I'm afraid you'll get sick again. I can't even say the C-word.

"I know that you get nightmares, but so do I." She looked at me. "I have a recurring nightmare where I'm an old lady, kind of a troll really, complete with a curved spine, and a mole on my nose." She hunched over and rounded her shoulders. "In my dream, I'm standing on the bridge of a castle, guarding a young princess, making sure that the dragon doesn't attack." She took a sip of her coffee. "I don't eat. I don't sleep. All I do is guard the castle." Tears filled the wrinkles of her crow's feet. "I have a weapon in my hand but in my dream, I can't see what it is. I stand there, poised for battle. Day after day, I watch for the dragon. If there's the slightest wind, or the sound of an animal, I aim by weapon. But…" She wiped her tears with the corner of her T-shirt. "…I never look up." She shrugged.

"Then my view zooms out and I'm in the clouds, looking down at myself. I'm pacing on the bridge. Right above the castle, there's a dragon flying around. He swoops low, dives toward the castle turret. He stretches his talons and snatches the princess from the turret window, and all I can do is watch him take her away." She paused. "It doesn't take a psychologist to figure that one out.

"So," she said. "You want to know why I make such a fuss about sunscreen and antibiotics? It's because I forgot to look up—I should have asked the doctors more questions."

"Maybe we should have all been asking more questions," I said. "The doctors, too."

"But I'm your mother."

"You're a great mother," I told her. "And if I were a dragon, I wouldn't want to fight you."

"Am I that bad?"

"You breathe fire, Mom."

"Sorry."

"Do *not* apologize," I said. "I like you being on my side."

"That I am."

"So in this dream, Mom, did I have long flowing blonde hair?"

"No, Miss Rapunzel, in my dream you are as beautiful as you are now."

I fingered my stubs of hair. "The next time you have that dream, could you give me long hair?"

"No," she said. "You're perfect just the way you are."

CHAPTER FIFTEEN

I was talking to Emi, and getting ready for Nate to come over at the same time.

"An all-girls' school? Are you crazy?" Emi wasn't keen on my idea of transferring to the Oahu School for Girls.

"Nobody would know me there." I squeezed the phone to my ear while I zipped my jeans. They were a little tighter. I was gaining back some weight.

"Rell, it's a small island. Of course someone would know you."

"But not everybody."

"You're right," Emi said. "No one would know a thing about you for maybe a week. But there are girls from Oahu School for Girls all over—as in some of them went to grammar school with us, as in Wanda Yamanaka spent a year there."

"You're right," I said.

"I'm always right," she said.

"Nowhere is safe. Maybe I'll transfer to the moon."

"No good," she said. "Some auntie would have a cousin whose son is an astronaut, and he would remember meeting you at a baby luau for your fifth-cousin."

"Hold on while I put my shirt on." I slipped on my *Dreamcatcher* shirt over my head. "I am never going back to Kailua High," I said. "I can't face anyone."

"You're being a baby. I'm not going to talk about this anymore. Tell me what you're wearing."

"My *Dreamcatchers* shirt and my jeans. My jeans are fitting better," I said.

"What time is Nate coming over?"

"At five."

At five o'clock, the doorbell rang; I was still in my room, putting my wig on.

Mom got to the door first. She hugged Nate. I never saw her hug him before, and I wasn't sure I was happy about it.

When I walked in the room, Mom and Nate both took a double take. They looked at my wig, but neither of them said anything about it.

"Hi," I said.

Nate brought me a bouquet of sunflowers tied with raffia. I hugged him, maybe he hugged me, I'm not sure.

"You're looking good, Rell." He gave me a thumbs-up. I remembered the first time he said me that. It was in the mall parking lot.

"Thanks," I said.

Enter my fantasy: I'm skipping through a field of sunflowers. My hair is trailing behind me. I'm wearing a see-through white dress that clings to my body. I run to Nate with my arms extended. He picks me up, lifts me in the air, and we twirl forever.

Enter reality. Nate said, "Your wig's nice."

It was probably the only thing he could think of to say.

"I wanted to you to notice me, not my gorgeous growing-in hair," I said.

He didn't answer.

"It looks lovely, Rell," Mom said. "With or without it, you're beautiful." Then Mom put her hand on Nate's shoulder. "Any big plans for the night?" she asked.

"Not really," Nate said.

"Can I entice the two of you to stay home with me and watch a video? I'll order in from that new Thai restaurant you and Emi went to," Mom said.

Sure, I thought. I've always wanted to share my date with my mother.

Nate and I exchanged glances. "I don't think so," he said.

"Sorry, Mrs. DeMello," Nate said. "I thought Rell and I would go to Gino's for dinner."

I was glad he hadn't totally gone over to Mom's side.

When we got to Gino's, the waitress seated us at a table right next to the window.

Nate pulled my chair out for me. "You do look terrific," he said.

"Thanks," I said.

"Emi told me she showed you how to put makeup."

I wondered what else she said. I imagined the two of them at the Honolulu General Hospital waiting room talking for seven straight hours.

Nate picked up his menu. "Do you know what you want to eat?" he asked me.

"Not yet."

I glanced out the window across the street toward the bowling alley. A family was pouring out of a full-sized van. There must have been ten of them. They were like ducks in a line, with bowling bags for wings. They waddled through the parking lot into Bowl-O-Rama.

When I looked back at Nate, he was staring at my wig.

"I don't want any extra attention tonight. Passing out at school was enough for a lifetime."

"Rell, it wasn't as bad as you make it out."

Sure, right in the middle of the red beans and chili rush, I roll my eyes back like a zombie and dive head first for the table.

"The waitress is coming." Nate folded his menu.

"You ready to order?" She pulled her order pad out of her waistband.

Nate ordered spaghetti and meatballs; I ordered Cheese Ravioli.

"Anything to drink?" the waitress asked.

"Diet Coke."

"And two glasses of water," Nate added.

Nate and I held hands across the table, flanking an empty, straw-covered bottle of Chianti with an unlit candle in it.

"My mother told me you were at the hospital until midnight."

I leaned back as the busboy poured our water. His shirt smelled like fried garlic, and he could have used some deodorant.

"I stayed for a while," Nate said.

"Thanks," I said

"It was no big deal."

"Emi told me you kept kids from coming around me after I passed out."

"Forget it, Rell. It's over. Just move on."

I got it. You pass out with the whole school watching, and you don't fall to your knees and cry. You don't change your name or move to a different city. You don't even drown yourself in a gallon of ice cream. You forget it and move on.

"You mom told me you're going to San Francisco to see LB," Nate said. "She thinks she should go with you."

"I'm a big girl," I said. "I can handle getting on a plane all by myself."

"Your mother is worried about you, Rell."

What happened at the hospital that night? Emi thinks Nate's a nice guy, and Nate has a case of Mother Worship.

"She's worried what it'll do to you if LB dies."

"You and my mother seem to be new best friends," I said.

"I'm just telling you what I think, Rell."

"I don't care what you think!"

I must have said it louder than I thought, because the guy at the next table turned around and looked at me. He was about forty, overweight, with eight strands of gray hair combed over his freckled scalp.

"Rell, I've got to tell you something before you go."

The bus boy brought over a basket of bread.

"I've been wanting to tell for a while," Nate said.

I was sure he was going to break up with me, and I wasn't so unhappy about it.

"Spaghetti?" The waitress held up a plate, and Nate told her it was his. "And ravioli." She put my food down in front of me.

I reached for a piece of bread, and Nate reached for my hand.

"Let go of my hand," I said.

"Listen to me," he said.

I looked out the window and wondered how the family of bowlers were doing.

"I've been reading about Hodgkin's disease," Nate said.

That was what he wanted to tell me?

"Why? Do you have some kind of Hodgkin's test you're studying for?"

"I want to know more about you."

"I'm not about Hodgkin's disease," I said.

"Okay," he said. "I wanted to know more about what you went through. How's that for a reason?"

Going out with Nate was a mistake.

I stared right past him. A gray-haired woman in a too-tight suit walked into the restaurant. The bald man at the table next to us stood up. The two of them hugged.

There's somebody for everyone.

"I read a few cancer survivor websites," Nate said.

"I am not a cancer survivor," I said.

"Rell, you had cancer, you were treated, and you survived. That makes you a cancer survivor."

Cold-hearted logic from the math geek.

"It's nothing to be ashamed of," he said.

"I'm not an anything-survivor," I said. "I'm just like everybody else, I just had cancer, that's all."

"So did I," Nate said.

He put his hand out as if he were introducing himself. "Nathan Y. S. Lee, T-cell lymphoma, Stage II, seventy weeks treatment."

I felt like I got the wind knocked out of me, like when I fell off the monkey bars on the playground and landed on my back.

"That's what I wanted to tell you."

"Why tell me now?" I asked.

"It's important."

The waitress stopped at our table. She asked if everything was all right.

"Just perfect," I answered. "My boyfriend just told me he's a cancer survivor."

"Oh," she said and high-tailed it away from us as soon as she could.

"That was really dumb," Nate said.

"Why? I thought being a cancer survivor was nothing to be ashamed of?"

"It was unfair to the waitress."

"Life's not fair. People keep telling me that over and over. Life's not fair. Get over cancer. Don't wear it like a merit badge. Just move on."

"I'm sorry. I wanted to tell you sooner."

"You say you're sorry when you bump into somebody, or when you step on their toe, not when you forget to tell them you had cancer."

"I wanted to tell you," he repeated.

And I wanted to be Miss America.

I could feel the tears welling in my eyes. I will not cry, I told myself. I will not cry. I will not make a scene. I told myself to think of something funny—anything. I thought about Ajax chasing his tail, about the magician at Emi's tenth birthday party, about my first bra, my first period, the first time I plucked my eyebrows—but the tears kept coming.

"How could you not tell me?" I asked.

"I wanted to. Honest."

I wiped my face with my napkin. The tears wouldn't stop.

"There never was a good time."

For a good time, call Rell DeMello. And make a fool of her while you're at it.

"Is that why you transferred from St. Luke's?" I asked.

"Partly."

"And the trips to San Francisco?"

"Follow-up tests."

"Nate, you lied to me."

"I didn't lie."

"You knew I had cancer," I said.

"Everybody knew you had cancer, Rell."

"Why didn't you tell me you did?"

"Because I didn't want you to feel sorry for me," he said.

"But it was all right for you to feel sorry for me?"

"What did you want me to say, Rell? Hi. My name is Nate Lee, I've had cancer. Do you want to go out with me? Tell the truth, Rell, would you have gone out with me if I told you?"

"Probably not," I said. "But you didn't give me a chance to decide."

"Once we started to go out, I wanted to tell you, but it was never the right time."

"Well, this is lousy timing, too," I said. "In the middle of Gino's eating ravioli."

"Do you want to leave?"

"No, I want to sit here and cry in my food."

Nate paid the bill and the two of us walked through the parking lot, slowly, not holding hands, not even walking close to each other. We got in the front seat of the truck and sat there.

"Why did you want to go out with me in the first place?" I asked.

"I don't know."

"Emi said that you went out with me to protect me."

"Maybe at first I did."

"There have to be guys at Kailua who knew you when you were at St. Luke's."

"There are."

"And they knew you had cancer, right?"

"Guys are different," he said. "And I didn't broadcast that I had it."

"You think I did!"

"That's not what I meant, Rell."

"Where were you treated in San Francisco?"

"I went to Stanhope when I got diagnosed, and the doctors there worked out my treatment. But I got treated at Honolulu General."

I remembered all the hospital parking stubs in his glove compartment.

"I've been out of treatment for two years and eight months. My follow-ups have been great since, then, but I had a scare last year and I had to go back to Stanhope to get it checked."

"Were you there when I was there?"

"I was an outpatient. Even if you were there, I wouldn't have seen you," he said.

"What happened with the scare?"

"It was nothing," he said. "But my parents told the school. My teachers knew what was going on and so did some of the guys I hung out with."

"How did the guys treat you?"

"At first they were freaked out. But once we did things like play basketball together, they forgot about it. I got in a few shots. They shoved me, I shoved them. Nobody cared," he said. "Guys don't make issues of things."

"So, cancer's a girl thing," I said. "All this time, all I had to do was shoot some hoops and every thing would be fine."

"Rell, guys *are* different."

"I know. Mr. Rogers explained it to me. Guys are prettier on the outside and girls are prettier on the inside."

Nate drummed the steering wheel with his fingers. "I haven't forgotten what happened to me, Rell. I just don't think about it."

"And how do you do that?"

"I keep it in a box."

Move on. Don't think about it. Keep it in a box.

"I guess I don't have strong enough wrapping tape."

"Rell, I'm not saying it hasn't changed me. It changed me a lot."

"How?"

"I don't wait for things to happen, I make them happen. I do things the first time they come around. I take risks."

"You're not the skydiving type," I said.

"Calculated risks."

Of course, everything can be reduced to numbers.

"After your treatment, what kind of survival odds did your doctor give you?" I asked.

"She told me that my cancer would probably never come back. But she wouldn't say 100%."

"And you're not afraid it will?"

"I focus on the 100%."

"I don't believe you."

"Rell, if I looked for cancer, I could find it every day." Nate put his back to the driver's side door and put his feet up on the seat. "I choose not to look for it."

"Truth or dare," I said.

"Truth," he answered.

"When you were sick, did you ever think you were going to die?"

"Sure."

"What did you think about?"

"I thought about all the things I would miss doing—like teaching my nephew Noah how to dribble. What did you think about?"

"I thought about how sad it would be for my mom and dad if I died. How they only had one child. How I would never get married or have a baby." I leaned back on the passenger door and faced him. "What do you think is stronger, hope or fear?"

"Whatever sees you through," Nate said.

I took his hand and pressed it against my neck. "Feel it?" I put his finger over the lump. "It's new," I said. "It's hard, it's round, and it doesn't move."

I took his hand down.

"So, what's stronger?" I asked. "Hope or fear?"

He didn't answer, he put his arm around me, and said, "When did you find it?"

"A couple of days ago."

"What did the doctors say?"

"I haven't told anyone yet."

"Not even your parents."

"You're the first."

"Rell, you know you have to get this checked," Nate said.

I nodded.

"Right away," he said.

"I know."

"When are you going to do it?"

"When I go to Stanhope, I'm going to ask Dr. Braden to take a look at it," I said.

"What about your parents?"

"I'm not telling them," I said. "I don't want to worry them."

"And you think your doctor is going to check you out without telling your parents?"

"Dr. Braden will do it. He's a good guy."

Chapter Sixteen

Early Sunday morning, Mom came in my room. "Mrs. O'Donnell called," she said.

I knew she was going to tell me that LB had died.

Mom sat down on my bed. "Mrs. O'Donnell said the doctors aren't sure LB will make it through the weekend."

She'll die without me there.

"Dad's rearranged your flight. You're leaving this afternoon," she said.

I said I wanted to be with LB when she died. I told myself and everybody I knew that, but I really didn't. I wished Dad would have left my flight alone, and I wouldn't have had to deal with LB's dying.

"I was supposed to go out with Emi today," I said.

"I'm sure she'll understand," Mom said.

"I know," I said. "But I've got to tell her I'm going."

Emi wasn't home. I assumed they were at church. They went to church every Sunday. At St. Mark's Methodist Church. In my family, we were Easter and Christmas Catholics.

I left two messages for her. One to ask her to call me back, and the other to tell her I was leaving. I was playing a game of solitaire on my computer when Emi walked into my room. She was carrying a three-foot-long box of flowers—orchids, ti leaf, ginger, and birds of paradise.

"The flowers are for LB from my parents," she said. "The chocolates." She pulled out a box of chocolate-covered macadamia chocolate from her purse. "Are for LB from me."

That was so nice of Emi's parents, I thought. The only way they knew LB was from stories I told Emi.

"Thanks." I hugged her. Her perfume smelled like watermelon.

"I don't know if LB can eat chocolate or not," Emi said. "But...."

"I'm sure she'll try some," I said, although I wasn't sure either.

Emi looked at my plaid suitcase on my bed. "Don't you have a bigger one?" It was bulging.

"That's the biggest I have."

"My parents have a huge rolly-bag they take to Vegas," she said. "If you want to borrow it, I can get it."

"It's okay, Em," I said and pulled out a smaller matching bag out of my closet. "I'll split up my stuff and I'll take the flowers as a carry-on." I fingered the cellophane window on the flower box. "They're gorgeous, Emi. LB's going to love them."

"I wish I could go with you, Rell."

"It's okay," I said.

I unzipped my suitcase and spilt my stuff, but even after I did, it took both Emi and me to hold them down to zip them closed.

"I could go the airport if you want me to," Emi said.

I nodded. "That would be great."

"It's going to be hard, isn't it?" Emi asked.

I started to cry. "Yup." I tried to smile. It was the only way I could keep from breaking down. "Real hard."

Dad came in and took my bags to the car. Mom was in the kitchen wrapping up cream cheese brownies for me to take to Dr. Braden.

As I walked to the car, Emi held my hand, as if we were kindergarten play friends. She held my hand as we drove to the airport, too, and a few times, she gave it a tight squeeze.

When we got to the United Airlines terminal, Nate was there.

"Your mom called me," he said. "She said it was okay if I came to the airport."

Mom and Dad got in the United line.

Emi handed Nate the box of flowers. "You two go through the Agriculture inspection," she said. "Rell, I'll stay with your parents."

Obviously, Emi wasn't try to keep Nate and me apart anymore.

Nate took the flowers and we waited in the Agriculture line. "It's going to be okay," he said. "You're stronger than you think, Rell."

Right. I come from a long line of Cabral and DeMello women.

"When it gets hard, think of LB."

That was exactly what I didn't want to do.

"You'll get through it, for her," he said.

"I don't want to go," I said.

"She's your friend, Rell. Who would want to watch a friend die?"

Point well taken.

"You'll be fine," he said.

I stared at the ceiling to keep my tears from falling. "I guess."

"Rell, did the node go away?" he asked.

"No." I shook my head.

"Promise me you'll get the node checked while you're there."

"I will," I said.

"And write down everything the doctor says."

"I will."

"And call me if you get bad news. Any time. No matter when."

I nodded.

"It's probably just a reactive node," he said. "Nothing to worry about."

That was Nate being scared to the bone.

"I know," I said.

Then he kissed me. Within eyesight of my parents, he kissed me. It was only a peck on the cheek.

For the next five hours on the plane, all I could think about was LB dying, and maybe me being the next to die.

When the plane landed at the San Francisco airport, a limousine driver was waiting for me in the baggage claim area. He was an older guy in a rumpled black suit. He was holding up a cardboard sign with big red felt tip letters. "Rell DeMello."

I felt like a corporate executive getting off the plane. I should have been carrying a computer and a leather attaché, instead of a box of flowers and two zipper-screaming plaid suitcases.

The driver loaded my luggage in the car and drove me to Stanhope's Hospitality House. The night clerk at the Hospitality House carried my bags down to my room. The room had two twin beds and a cot. Each bed was covered with a different print spread. The bathroom had jumbles of donated hotel soaps, and the coffee table was stacked with old magazines.

On the nightstand was a red vinyl binder filled with handwritten notes—tips and encouragement from families who stayed in the room before. It was just like the room my mother and I stayed in while I was in treatment.

I remembered unpacking the first time I stayed there. I was hoping that my cancer diagnosis was a mistake, and the doctors at Stanhope would take tests and send me home, say that my lump was a swollen gland. I was hoping Dr. Braden would say that to me this time, too.

I settled in, and called LB's hospital room phone.

Mrs. O'Donnell answered the phone. "Oh, Rell. It's so good to hear your voice."

Mrs. O'Donnell sounded tired and her sentences were filled with sighs. She apologized for not being at the airport to welcome me, then she apologized for not being at the Hospitality House. Then she asked me if I was hungry. "I could send Mr. O'Donnell over with some food," she said.

"No, Mrs. O'Donnell," I said. "I'm really not hungry."

Mrs. O'Donnell told me that LB looked different from the last time I saw her. "She's lost considerable weight," she said. "And she's in pain most of the time." Mrs. O'Donnell took in a long breath. "Last night she had a chest tube put in, and she's on a morphine drip."

The more I heard, the more I wanted to go home.

"If it gets too hard for you to be with her, Rell, we will all understand."

There was nothing to say.

"Elizabeth's asleep for the night," Mrs. O'Donnell said. "She had her meds about an hour ago. She wouldn't know if you were here. So get some sleep, and I'll call you in the morning."

"The flight did wipe me out," I said.

"Mr. O'Donnell or I will pick you up in the morning, and drive you over."

The Hospitality House was a half-mile from the hospital. It was certainly within walking distance for me.

"If you need anything before then, just call. One of us will be here all night."

I pictured them sitting next to LB's bed. I imagined LB with a tube in her chest, IVs in her arm, asleep, while her parents kept vigil.

I couldn't say it, and hated thinking it, but in the deepest part of my soul, I wanted LB to die in the middle of the night so I wouldn't have to be with her.

I hung up the phone and sat on the bed and looked around the room. I remembered how my mother set up our room when we were there. She put her computer on the dresser, and scavenged cinderblocks and wood to make shelves for her books. She used the ironing board for her files and taught three classes from that room. It was her office and our home.

There were always wild flowers in a glass. And on the nights I slept there, she ordered in pizza, and we ate it straight out of the box, sitting cross-legged on the bed, watching TV.

I missed my mother. I looked over at the empty bed next to me and wished I had let her come with me. If she were here, she'd be telling me to get ready for bed and take a shower.

I did take a shower. I ran my fingers down my neck. The node on my neck felt bigger.

The next morning, I wore my long-sleeved yellow top and my Hat-Hair wig. I grabbed the chocolates, the flowers, mom's home made brownies, and I walked to the hospital, through the front entrance, past the gift shop, the chapel, past the cafeteria, the barber and the post office. It was all familiar—doctors being paged, deliverymen carrying bouquets, orderlies wheeling around patients.

In the elevator to the seventh floor, there was a woman in a wheelchair with a portable respirator. I squeezed in between her and the volunteer who was escorting her.

"Seventh floor," I said, knowing that volunteer would know that the seventh floor was the Pediatric Oncology Unit.

I checked myself out in the smoked glass elevator wall. I smiled. My Hat-Hair wig looked natural. I was carrying in candy and flowers. It made me look like a visitor, not a patient.

I got out at the seventh floor and turned left. I was back. I couldn't move. Straight ahead of me were the red iron "castle" gates to the unit. I was back.

A Red Cross lady asked me if I was lost.

"No." I shook my head.

I swung open the castle gates and walked past the mural of kings and queens and rabbits and deer. Two little boys raced down the hall on plastic tricycles. I knew that, any second, a nurse would appear and put them on "time out."

I walked to the nurses' station and checked the patient board. "Elizabeth O'Donnell. Room 7-12." She was still in our room.

I stood at the door.

LB was asleep. Mr. O'Donnell noticed me and waved me in.

"Rell." He got up and gave me a bear hug that almost lifted me off my toes. "Great to see you, kiddo." His beard bristled against my face. "You are quite the young lady," he said.

He let go of me and I caught my balance.

"Let me look at you," he said.

I held the box of chocolates and the flowers in the air, and I spun around.

"You look wonderful, kiddo."

"Thanks."

"Whatcha got there?" He pointed to the stuff I was carrying.

"Flowers from Hawaii," I said. "They're for you and Mrs. O'Donnell from my friend Emi's parents."

"And chocolate-covered macadamia nuts!" He took the box from me. "You remembered. My favorites."

Actually, I never knew he liked them, but I said. "Yup. Special delivery just for you, Mr. O'Donnell." I figured Emi couldn't eat them.

"Rell, it means so much to Mrs. O'Donnell and me that you're here."

Mr. O'Donnell had bags under his eyes, and his beard was a three-day old stubble.

"You look healthy, Rell."

It was the nicest thing a cancer-dad could have said to me, and it made me feel guilty.

"Let me get these flowers in water," I said, and I took the box from him.

When I checked around in the bathroom cabinet for something to use as a vase, I breathed in the smells—the Phisodex, the bleached hospital towels. It all came back—the alcohol smell, the antiseptics, the wax on the linoleum floor.

I found a glass flower vase under the sink and put the bouquet on LB's night stand.

"Hi, Roomie," LB said.

"Hey."

It was a good thing that Mrs. O'Donnell warned me about LB having lost weight. Her cheekbones were hallowed out and her eyes looked sunk in.

Such big eyes you have, Grandma.

I sat on the chair next to her bed. I lifted a tube coming from LB's chest over the back of the chair, and I sat cross-legged, so I could be higher, and closer to her. The noise from the drainage tube was loud, like slurping from a giant straw, and the liquid in the tub was cloudy.

Mr. O'Donnell stood at the foot of LB's bed.

"Elizabeth, I'm going down to the cafeteria to let Mom know that Rell's here. Do you want anything, Baby?"

"No, thanks." Her voice was a whisper.

"What about you, Rell?"

"An egg burrito and an OJ would be great," I said.

"Can do," he said and threw a kiss to LB.

"How are you doing, Elizabeth?" I was so used to her being LB that it sounded like a spoof when her dad called her by her real name.

"I've had better days, Estrella." She smiled.

"You want some water?" There was a blue plastic pitcher on her nightstand.

She shook her head.

I noticed her click the control of the IV dispenser to get a dose of morphine.

"It's for my chest," she said. "They put in a drainage tube yesterday. It's hard to breathe."

I noticed bloodstains on her pillow, and suspected they were from nosebleeds.

"Rell! I heard you were coming to visit us." It was Mrs. Norman. Mrs. Norman was one of the day-nurses. "How are you doing, girl?" She held me close and squeezed me to her king-sized-pillow breasts.

I pulled back my head to keep my wig from getting caught in her arms.

"Let me see you." She stood back and twirled her hand in the air.

One more spin of my body.

"You're filling out quite nicely, young lady." Mrs. Normal always smelled like baby powder. "I've heard you got yourself a boyfriend."

"Yes, Ma'am." After two minutes of being with Mrs. Norman, I fell into her North Carolina accent. "How did you know about my boyfriend?" I turned around and squinted my eyes at LB.

"I had to tell her," LB said.

"It's big news around here," Mrs. Norman said, then told me to stand up so she could check LB's IV.

"I heard your beau is cute and smart." She adjusted the couplings on LB's chest tube.

"He's not really my boyfriend."

"Rell," Dr. Braden said. He was in his green surgical scrubs, a sunflower cap, and paper shoe booties. "How's my favorite Hawaii patient?"

It was what he always said, and I said what I always said: "I'm your only Hawaii patient."

"It doesn't matter," he said. He opened his arms and I hugged him, resting my cheek on his chest.

"You look well."

"Thanks." I hoped he was going to tell me I was well, but that would come later.

"How's your mother?" Dr. Braden walked behind Mrs. Norman and checked LB's tubes, too.

"She made you cream cheese brownies." I got them out of my purse.

"One million thanks to your mother." He smiled.

Except for his gray hair, Dr. Braden looked like a college football player. He had broad shoulders, a wide square jaw, and intensely blue eyes the color of a cat's eye marble.

"How's school?" He asked as he made notes in LB's chart.

"A little rough at first, but it's getting easier."

"I heard you have a boyfriend."

I looked at LB.

"Was it on the PA?"

"Sorry," she said.

"We're more like friends," I told Dr. Braden.

"Does your friend get good grades?" he asked.

"He's the National Honor Society President."

"That's a good start," Dr. Braden said. "How about you? How are your grades?"

Mrs. Norman said, "Just leave the girl alone. You know she's got good sense."

"And you, Mrs. Norman, are beginning to sound more and more like my wife." He took his stethoscope out of his pocket and swung it around his neck. "Rell, do you mind giving me a little time alone with LB?"

"Yup." I knew the routine. "I'll be right outside." I waved to LB and stepped into the hall. I leaned my head against the tile, shut my eyes, and let all the air out of my lungs. I felt as if I just crossed the finish line of a marathon.

I wished I had never gone.

"Rell!" I heard Mrs. Spencer call me. Mrs. Spencer was Jason's mom. He had an early stage of neuroblastoma.

She gave me a hug. "Rell, no one told me you were coming. You look wonderful."

"Thanks."

"Are you back for follow-up testing?"

"No, to see LB."

"She's having a tough time of it," Mrs. Spencer said.

I nodded.

"It's so good to see you." She put her arm around me. "You've got to come down to see Jason." She walked me down to his room.

"How's he doing?" I asked her.

"Doctor Lynch said he's responding well. Two more treatments and he should be ready to go home." She swung open the door to Jason's room. "Jas, look who's here."

Jason was sitting up in bed watching his *All About Airplanes* video, probably for the two-hundredth time.

"Smelly Relly," he said.

"It's been a long time since I've heard that," I said. I walked over to his bed, hunched over. I made my hands into claws, and bared my teeth. "I'm going to get you!" I growled. "Ja-son." I crept closer.

"No, you won't!" He screamed and billowed his sheets and scrambled under them.

"Ja-son!" I snarled my lips.

He didn't move.

"Ja-son."

He peeked out from under his sheets. He took aim with his finger and "shot" me. "I zapped you with my monster power. You're dead," he said.

I clutched my chest, stood on my tiptoes, pivoted, and fell to the floor. "You got me, Big Boy."

Jason knelt up straight and beat his chest like a gorilla. His catheter protruded from his pajama tops.

When I stood up, he said, "Rell, you still don't know how to die very well."

I put my hands on my hips. "Says who?"

"Says me." He pushed back his sheets and said, "This is how you died." He rolled on his back, bicycled his leg in the air, then flopped on his mattress and shimmied like griddle-cooked bacon.

"Next time, I'll do it better," I said. I leaned over to hug him.

"Rell, you've got hair." He pointed to my Hat-Hair wig.

"Not this, but look." I lifted my wig to show him my real springs underneath it. "It's coming in," I said.

"Let me see." Mrs. Spencer came closer. "You are a regular long-haired beauty." She handed me a Play-Toy mirror. "Look at yourself."

The Rell I saw had thick eyebrows, pink skin, and deep brown eyes flecked with gold.

I did look good, and I looked healthy.

"Rell, there's an eight-year-old girl who just got diagnosed with Hodgkin's in 7-18. She's here this week for her first go round of treatment. Maybe you could stop by?"

"And show her the 'after' picture?" I asked.

"Her name is Allyson."

That's when it hit me. I was one of the "returning patients" who came to visit the unit when I was in treatment. They were the kids who brought in candy, and cookies, and pictures from their proms. They were the kids who were "cured"—the kids who were normal again.

Mr. O'Donnell peeked his head into Jason's room. He held up a cafeteria bag. "One egg burrito with OJ," he said.

"Thanks," I said, and turned to Jason. "See you later, Jas. Okay?"

As we were walking back to LB's room, Dr. Braden asked Mr. O'Donnell if he could speak to him. That was never good, and we all knew it.

The two of them went into Dr. Braden's office, and I went in to see LB alone.

LB was sipping water out of a squeeze bottle. "You really do look great, Rell."

"I must have looked awful before," I said.

"Terrific makeup," she said.

"My friend Emi showed me how to do it," I said. "I wrote to you about it. Remember?"

She shook her head. "It sounded like so much fun."

"It was no big deal," I said. I didn't want to tell her too many happy things, and make her feel bad about not doing "normal" stuff.

"What about your boyfriend?" She grinned.

"Things have changed," I said.

"Good-changed or bad-changed?"

"Just different."

LB clicked the morphine dispenser again.

"Do you have a limit on that stuff?" I asked.

"It's set high," she said. "I get a hit every time I click it."

I settled in the chair, and unwrapped my egg burrito. "Want some?" I offered.

"I don't eat much," she said.

I asked her about the new crop of interns.

"The cutest is Dr. Wallace," she said. "He's a redhead with braces on his teeth. And there's a female doc, Dr. Corky. She's really nice. Last Friday night she came in on her own time and watched a movie with me."

"Cool."

"Yeah. She got some wrapping paper for me, too." LB pointed to her dresser. "Rell, in the top drawer, there's a small box. Could you get it?"

I got it.

"Open it," she said. "It's for you."

The box was from The Mule Shop in the Grand Canyon. Inside was LB's fire agate stone.

"My mom had it turned into a necklace for you," she said.

The stone had flecks of gold and streaks of purple, and smoky gray. It was on silver chain.

"I won't be needing it," LB said. "It would have been a great trip, Rell."

I almost said that we would go, that she had to have hope, that this was just a set back. But we both were past pretending.

"Read the brochure," she said.

I wiped my tears to read it. "The fire agate is a stone known for its healing poperties. Shamans have held it during meditation because of its calming effects on the spirits. It is recommended to be worn as a talisman for healing."

"Sometimes the magic works. Sometimes it doesn't." LB shrugged.

I was afraid to hug her. She looked so frail. I put my arms around her shoulders, hoping I wasn't hurting her.

"I'm scared, Rell." She was crying.

I pressed my cheek to hers. There were her tears and mine. And we held each other. I didn't want to let go.

"Don't give up on miracles," I said.

"It's the only thing I have left," LB said.

I was sure if I let her go, she was going to die, right then.

"I'm going to miss you so much," I whispered.

"Right back at you, Roomie," she answered. Then she let go of me and said, "Put it on, Rell."

I squatted with my back to LB so she could hook the clasp.

"I'll never take it off," I said.

I turned around so she could see what it looked like.

"The magic's going to work for you, Rell. You're going to beat the dragon."

I wasn't sure.

Mr. O'Donnell came in. "Hey Baby," he said. "I brought you a strawberry banana shake." His eyes were red and puffy.

"Thanks, Dad, but I'm not hungry."

"This isn't for hungry. This is for fun," he said. "Take three sips and it's guaranteed to tickle your tummy like a tail thumping bunny."

"Oh, that was bad, Dad." LB groaned.

"It was great," he said. "You just don't have a well-developed sense of humor."

He got LB to laugh.

I asked Mr. O'Donnell if Dr. Braden was still on the floor.

"He's at the nurses' station," Mr. O'Donnell told me.

"Excuse me, for a sec, LB," I said. "I want to catch him before he leaves."

"See what your bad jokes do to my friends, Dad?" LB said. "They go running from the room."

"Don't worry, Rell, I've got a lot worse jokes for when you get back."

CHAPTER SEVENTEEN

I asked Dr. Braden if he had a minute to talk to me.

"Sure. What's up?"

"Can we go somewhere private to talk?" I didn't want to talk to him in the hall.

"My office?"

I nodded, and he walked me down the hall.

"What can I do for you, Rell?" he asked.

"Any word on the numbers?" I asked.

When I was in treatment, I would ask him that question when I wanted to know the newest studies on kids with Hodgkin's disease. I wanted to know the numbers—the survival rate numbers for kids who were being given the same drugs that I was.

The drugs I had been given were a new treatment. An experimental cocktail cooked up by the cancer center doctors at the University of South Florida.

"I read a report about two weeks ago that said Stage IIA event-free survival rates were about 92% after five years."

Event-free meant that no other cancers popped up, not even the kind that develop as a result of the chemotherapy drugs.

"It was a good choice," Dr. Braden said.

"Maybe not good enough."

"What do you mean?"

"I have a new node," I said.

"Where?"

"On my neck." I rubbed my finger over it. "It's small but it's hard, and it doesn't move."

"Have you seen Dr. Brice?" he asked.

Dr. Brice was the pediatric oncologist at Honolulu General.

I shook my head. "I wanted you to look at it first."

"Did your parents tell Dr. Brice I would be looking at you?"

"I didn't tell them."

"They don't know?"

I shook my head.

Dr. Braden swiveled his chair toward me. He rested his hands on his knees. "How long have you noticed it?"

"Maybe a week."

"Rell, you should have told your parents right away. You know that."

"I didn't want to worry them. I figured you'd take a look, and if it's nothing, they'd never have to know."

"Rell, this is your life we're talking about."

"All I want you to do is feel the node."

"I can't. Not without your parents' permission."

"It doesn't have to be anything official. Just feel my neck."

He reached for the phone. "What's your home number? I can call you mom now, and we can take care of the paperwork later."

I pushed his hand down. "Don't" I started crying. "Don't."

He put the phone down.

"I don't want them to know—not yet."

"Have you had any symptoms?" he asked.

"Nothing," I said.

"Night sweats? Fever? Rashes?"

"No."

"Your weight looks good," he said.

"There's nothing wrong with me but the node," I said.

Dr. Braden's pager went off. He checked it and said. "I'm going to have to tell your parents, Rell."

I thought I could trust him.

"Why?"

"I have to inform them." His pager went off again.

"I'll tell them. I promise," I said.

"When are you leaving for Hawaii?"

"The day after tomorrow."

"Rell, if you have relapsed, you need to be here. You need to be tested."

"Biopsies?"

"Probably." His pager went off a third time.

"Do you think my cancer is back?" I asked him.

"I can't tell with just a physical examination, Rell."

"Then why won't you do it?"

"If I talk to your parents, I will," he said. "But not without them knowing. It's out of the question, Rell."

"All I want you to do is feel the node."

"This isn't a game, Rell." He stood up, and checked his pager again. "You call your parents today, and I'll see what we can set up."

"Okay," I said.

He stood up, and walked me down the hall.

When I went back to LB's, Mrs. O'Donnell was standing in the hall.

"Rell." She took me into her arms. "Thank you for coming." It was the first time I had seen her since I left Stanhope. She looked paler and thinner. She wasn't wearing any makeup and her black hair had gray roots.

"Are you okay, Mrs. O'Donnell?" I asked.

"Dr. Braden just gave us some bad news," she said. "The cancer has spread to Elizabeth's spine. It's in the base of her skull."

"It's in her spine," I repeated her words and I nodded my head as if I were a bobble-head doll.

"Does she know?" I asked.

"Her father and I just told her."

I tried not to let the truth in.

"Rell, I can't believe this is happening." Mrs. O'Donnell twisted a tissue between her fingers. "I kept telling myself that she was going to beat this thing. I really believed it."

I put my arms around her and she sobbed, burying her head against my shoulder. She was an adult, crying in my arms.

"I've got to stop this," she said firmly and pulled back. She pushed her hair back. "I can't fall apart. Not now," she said "I need to hang tough."

Why?

"I don't want Elizabeth to see me like this."

Do you think she doesn't know how your feeling?

When I went into LB's room, her eyes were closed. Whether she was asleep or just closing herself off to the world, it didn't matter.

LB and I were alone. I sat, watching her breathe—quick, shallow gasps, almost a pant. My eyes were glued to her chest. I matched my breathing to hers, as if I were breathing for her. I breathed to keep her alive.

LB opened her eyes. "I'm not going to make it, Rell."

Where were all the angels of mercy that guarded the souls of children?

"I'm not afraid of being dead," LB said. "I'm afraid of dying."

I could feel tears pouring down my cheeks.

"Miracles happen." I wanted to play the game of hope until her last dying breath. "You have to have hope."

"I'm going to die hoping," she said. Then she closed her eyes and drifted to sleep.

I sat down next to her, curled my legs up, and wrapped myself in the blanket as tight as I could.

Where are you, God?

LB's body looked as if her body gave up and only her spirit was keeping her alive. LB once told me that she thought we were the lucky ones—all of us in the cancer unit—because we were the ones who knew we had cancer and were getting treatment. While the other kids who thought they were normal, didn't know they had it, and the disease was eating them alive.

I hated cancer and I hated a God that let it happen. Mrs. Norman used to tell us that God takes back his most special angels to be close to him.

What kind of selfish God would do that? I hated that God, and I hated pictures of him sitting on a rock with little kids around him, because I knew that all those little kids were dead.

LB was going to die; it was a fact. I wished that I had special words to say to her—like some poem with words so beautiful that they should be written with pure gold. But I couldn't work on some movie farewell, I was just trying to force myself not to run out of the room.

When LB's parents came back, they plumped up her pillow, they adjusted her bed, filled her pitcher with water, smoothed out her sheets. Mr. O'Donnell paced with his hands in his pockets, rattling his loose change. Mrs. O'Donnell folded towels. LB slept, unaware.

I remembered my mother folding towels in my hospital room. She smoothed my sheets, and plumped up my pillow. She filled my water pitcher, and adjusted the window shades to keep the sun out of my eyes, and it made me mad that she had to clean house, even in the hospital. I wanted to scream at her that I have cancer, and you're going around like Mrs. Clean. But watching Mrs. O'Donnell go from one chore to another, I began to understand how it must have been for my mother.

I needed a break from sitting with LB.

I never wanted to see another hospital room again. I walked down the hall, strolled through the lobby, sat in the chapel, and browsed the gift shop, before going to the cafeteria.

All hospital cafeterias are the same—tables of people wearing scrubs, discussing patients while they eat, doctors jumping up when their names are paged, patients in wheelchairs dragging IV poles behind them, families huddled together, families quiet, families not knowing what was going to happen next.

I got in line and slid my tray across the stainless steel tube shelf, past counters of deep-fried chicken and heat-lamp kiosks of rubbery pizza. I ordered a salad. It had brown-tinged lettuce leaves and hard yellow-orange tomatoes. I poured myself a Diet Coke.

I sat at a far table next to the window. Outside there was a girl sitting in a wheel chair trimmed with Mylar ribbon. The girl looked like Tess. She was wearing a tie-dyed turban on her head.

Right after Tess died, I was sure I saw her alive. I thought she was a patient in the radiation clinic, but she wasn't. Once I thought I saw her at the Laundromat at the Hospitality House. After a while, it stopped happening. After a little while longer, it was hard to picture her face. I didn't want LB to fade away like that. I didn't want her to die.

Chapter Eighteen

I walked the grounds of the hospital until dusk; then I went back to my room. I was still jet-lagged and had no sense of time. I turned on the TV but don't remember what I watched.

There were two messages on the phone. My mother called twice. Nate called once.

I didn't call either one of them.

I fell asleep with the TV on, and I dreamed about LB. The two of us were swirling through banners of yellow and green. A banjo played, a fiddler called out steps. LB and I were locked arm-in-arm, dancing, and spinning to the music.

The fiddler called, "Faster the flute. Faster the banjo. Faster the fiddler's thumb." A young girl sang, "Throw over the veil. Throw open the sky. Your friend has gone to God."

I woke up panting.

My heart pounded. It was three a.m. I was afraid to call LB's room, because I was sure that she was dead. I dialed my house to talk to my mother. But when I realized it was midnight, I hung up.

When I did see LB the next morning, I found out that during the night LB had seizures. I was sitting next to her that morning when she had another one. I watched her body shake. Her mother ran for the nurse. Her father held her shoulders down.

"Hold on," I whispered. "Hold on."

Two nurses ran in. LB's body convulsed one more time. Then she was quiet.

Please, God. Not now.

I didn't want to see what the nurses were going to do to her. I couldn't watch anymore.

I stood in the hallway, leaned against the tile walls, and let myself slide to the floor until I was crouched with my knees to my chest.

An intern ran by me, into LB's room. A real doctor was behind him, and then Mrs. Norman.

I could hear them calling out orders to each other.

Please God, make it all go away, I prayed.

Mrs. Norman was first to come out. She put her arms around me.

"Is she alive?" I asked.

"She's a tough little angel," Mrs. Norman said. "She made it." She told me that LB's seizures were "to be expected" with the drugs they giving her. They were "hitting the cancer" with everything they had. *But it was the patient who died in the crossfire.*

Mrs. Norman said the seizures would become more frequent.

I didn't want LB to die like that—with her body shaking, and everyone rushing around her. I wanted it to be peaceful.

LB lay in her bed. Her body rattled a few more times while she slept.

I sat next to her for so long, my legs fell asleep. I walked off the needles and pins, slapping them as I walked. I walked in circles next to LB's bed, and noticed an index card on her bed stand. It was a poem by Carl Sandburg.

> *Loosen your hands,*
> *Let go and say goodbye.*
> *Let the stars and the songs go.*
> *Loosen your hands and say goodbye.*

I didn't want to loosen my hands or let go. I wanted to tear the stars out of the sky, and wrap them up in a bouquet, and give it to LB and Tess.

On my last day at Stanhope, LB's energy soared. She was sitting up, telling jokes, laughing. It terrified me, because right before Tess died, she rallied, too.

Mrs. O'Donnell ordered deep-dish pizza from Aunty Caroline's.

"Do I smell pizza?" Jason's mom said, as she wheeled Jason into LB's room.

"Pizza," Jason squealed. "Pizz-ah, feast-ah!" Jason had discovered rhyming.

His mom tied a blue plastic bib over his pajamas—his chemo port had to be covered.

"Dad got a personal-sized mushroom and sausage pizza just for you, Rell," LB said. "The one with the anchovies is for Mrs. Norman."

We sat around LB's room and laughed and ate and wiped streaks of tomato sauce off our cheeks. I took a bite of my pizza, stretching the cheese out to the ceiling. "Aunty Caroline makes the best pizza in the world. Too bad she doesn't deliver to Hawaii."

"Can you imagine it, Rell?" Mr. O'Donnell said. "One thousand 'plane pizzas' to go." He extended his arm out like airplane wings and tilted them to the right. "Get it? *Plane* pizzas?"

We all groaned. Mr. O'Donnell beamed.

We were joking, as if we were normal people. As if we were sitting around LB's house and the delivery boy dropped off pizzas.

I checked my watch. It was getting closer to the time I had to leave. LB checked the wall clock. About ten minutes before I had to go, LB's mom cleared everyone but me out of the room.

I held LB's hand.

"Promise me you'll get to the Grand Canyon, Rell."

"Absolutely," I said.

"And hike all the way to the bottom."

"Can I take a tour bus?" I asked.

"You hike. And you think of me every step of the way."

"I can think of you in an air-conditioned bus," I said.

"No. And promise me that you'll tell me all about it. And tell me about school, and Nate, and Emi. And when you get married, and have babies, I want to know every detail of that, too. Even if you think I can't hear you, I'll be listening." She started to cry and cupped her hand over her face. "Do you remember what it was like to cry without eyelashes?" She was both crying and laughing.

I grinned and nodded.

"You know the worst part, Rell? I'll never know what was supposed to happen to me. I wish I could fast-forward my life, just to find out, and then rewind it back to now. I just want to know."

"I love you, LB," I said.

"Right back at you, Roomie."

Those were the last words she said to me.

Before leaving for the hospital, I stopped by to see Dr. Braden. There was a young doctor waiting in his office. He had red hair and braces.

It must be the new intern, I thought.

"Hi," I said."

"Hi. I'm Dr. Wallace."

I asked him if Dr. Braden were around.

"He should be here soon," he told me. "We're supposed to discuss one of my patients."

"One of his patients"— he definitely was an intern.

"I used to be a patient of Dr. Braden's," I said. "Hodgkin's disease. Stage IIA." They always wanted to know your diagnosis. "I've been back here a few days."

"Have you relapsed?" he asked.

I almost said no, but then, I thought about it. I figured if he thought I had relapsed, I could get him to check my neck.

"A couple of weeks ago," I said. "I have a node in my neck." I put my finger over where the node was. "Do you want to feel it?" Interns loved to make their own diagnoses.

He stood in front of me and ran his fingers over the node. He had a gentle touch, not typical of interns. Then he felt under my jaw, behind my ears and down my collarbone.

"Did you feel it?"

"Here." He put his finger right over it.

"That's it," I said.

"It feels suspicious," he said.

"Dr. Wallace!" Dr. Braden walked in.

The intern took his hands off me. He stood up. "Sir?"

"Wait for me in the conference room."

Dr. Wallace looked as afraid as I was.

I knew what I did was bad, beyond bad, maybe illegal, but I didn't care.

"Don't get mad at him," I told Dr. Braden. "It was my fault."

"I'll deal with him later, Rell."

"I tricked him."

"Just exactly what did you think would happen?" Dr. Braden sat in his chair, facing me.

"I wanted somebody to check my node," I said, "And you wouldn't do it." As soon as I said it, I knew I crossed the line.

He reached for the phone. "Rell, what's your phone number?"

I didn't answer him.

"It's in the computer, Rell," he said. "Save me the time of getting it."

I told him the number and he called my house. My mother answered, and I listened as he told her what I had just done. The last thing he said to her was, "I'll take a look at her right now."

"Come on, Rell. You're going to get your wish." He escorted me into an examination room.

I lied down on the table and closed my eyes. I didn't want to look at him. I knew what I did was wrong, but if he had just felt my neck to begin with, none of this would have happened.

"Right here?"

"Yes."

"Swallow," he said, and I did. "Swallow again." I swallowed again.

"Turn your head to the left, please," he said.

"Turn your head to the right," he told me.

"Is it back?" I asked.

"I can't say without more tests."

It was back.

"What now?" I asked him.

"I'm going to call Dr. Brice about doing some tests. I won't say anything more, Rell."

My flight back to Honolulu arrived at three o'clock in the afternoon. We went directly from the airport to Honolulu General Hospital. The ride over was uneasy. It was as if Mom and Dad were forged together as a team—fighting cancer and being angry with me.

It was different from when I was first diagnosed. This time we all knew what we were facing.

The three of us got in the elevator. We walked down the hall into the Pediatric Oncology Clinic, and we sat in three chairs in a line, blue tweed chairs that were bolted to the floor. CNN was on TV. They were covering the war; there was always a war.

Next to the TV was a photo collage of the "Cancer Hall of Fame." I remembered the first time I saw it. It was when my family doctor sent me to see Dr. Brice because he suspected that I had cancer.

I remembered looking at the photos, thinking that my photo didn't belong on that board. That was a board for kids who were going to die. My photo still wasn't up there—it was at Stanhope on a board just like it.

I got up and looked over the photos of the kids. Girls, boys, little kids teens. Everyone of them was smiling—including Nate Lee.

Dr. Brice welcomed us into his office. Dr. Brice was about seventy. He had steel-gray eyes and a tight gray crew cut. He wore a white lab coat, a blue shirt, and a maroon-and-gold striped tie. Most of the other doctors at Honolulu General wore Aloha shirts under their lab coats.

"This is Dr. Alaire," he introduced us to a young woman standing behind his desk.

"She's a pediatric-oncology resident."

Dr. Alaire had wavy auburn hair pulled back in a French braid. She had green eyes and a kind smile.

Dr. Brice talked in a matter-of-fact voice. "I have spoken at length with Dr. Braden." He flipped through papers in a manila folder. "Estrella's last tests results were all within normal limits. Her health is good and her blood work has consistently been excellent."

I held on to LB's agate stone, while Dr. Brice shifted the papers in the folder.

"Dr. Braden and I are in agreement that an FNA should be the next step."

Mom nodded. Dad asked what an FNA was.

"Fine needle aspiration," Dr. Brice explained. "It's a simple procedure where we insert a needle into the node and extract cells from it." Dr. Brice folded his hands as he spoke. His hands were old and gnarled, and covered with age spots. I was hoping that a younger doctor would do the biopsy.

"It's done with a topical anesthetic. It's quite painless."

"When will you do it?" Dad asked.

"We have it scheduled for tomorrow morning at seven."

Dad crossed his legs. He tapped his thigh with his thumb. "When do we get the results?"

"The next day," Dr. Brice said.

Dad jiggled his foot. "Do you think this is cancer?" That was Dad taking the direct approach.

"Mr. DeMello, girls Estrella's age commonly have swollen lymph nodes. Most of them are never noticed, and within a few weeks, they're gone. However, given Estrella's medical history, it's best to take an aggressive approach with testing."

"What are you saying? Is it cancer or not?" Dad needed guarantees.

"We don't know," Dr. Brice answered.

"I thought Hodgkin's disease was a curable cancer," Dad said.

"We have been quite successful in treating Hodgkin's disease. Yes."

"You know Rell was treated at Stanhope," Dad said. "It's one of the best hospitals in the world for treating Hodgkin's."

He knows that Dad, and he knows you just slammed him and every doctor at Honolulu General.

"Mr. DeMello, despite our best efforts, sometimes patients relapse."

Mom reached for Dad's hand.

"May I?" Dr. Alaire asked Dr. Brice; he nodded.

"Mr. DeMello," Dr. Alaire said. "The prognosis for pediatric Hodgkin's patients is excellent. Even if Estrella has relapsed, her prognosis would still be quite good."

That was the wrong thing to say to my father.

"It can't be back," my father declared it. It must be so.

"For all we know," Dr. Alaire said. "This could be a reactive node. Nothing to worry about."

She smiled at me. I smiled back. Dad wasn't smiling.

"So, Estrella, why don't we get started?" Dr. Alaire said.

She led me to an examining room and readied me for Dr. Brice.

"Do you prefer being called Rell?" she asked.

"Uh-huh." I knew she was trying to get me to relax.

When Dr. Brice came in, he told Dr. Alaire to examine me, while he supervised her every move. Then he checked me.

I watched as the two of them worked. I was looking for any clue as to what either of them thought—a surprised look, a pitying glance, a momentary stare between the two of them—any sign to tell me if they thought my cancer was back.

"Okay, Rell," Dr. Alaire said. "We're finished for today. We'll see you bright and early tomorrow morning."

I got dressed and went back into the waiting room. Mom and Dad jumped up like jacks-in-the-box.

Dad put his arm around me. "Whatever happens, we'll get through this. All of us. One step at a time."

We were going to face cancer as a family.

That night I called Nate. I expected him to say he would be right over, that he would bring me flowers, and hold me, and tell me everything would be all right. I wanted him to tell me not to worry, that these nodes are normal. But he didn't.

When I told him I tricked an intern into examining my neck, he said, "I can't believe you pulled a stunt like that. What were you thinking? Talking to an intern? You know more about cancer than any intern."

"I wanted someone to examine me," I told him.

"What did Dr. Braden do?"

"He called my mother. I didn't think he would do that."

"What did you expect him to do, Rell?" I could picture Nate shaking his head, disgusted by my illogic. "What happens next?"

"I'm scheduled for an FNA in the morning."

"Why an FNA?" Nate asked. "You need to get that whole thing cut out."

"The docs don't think it's necessary."

"You need a second opinion, Rell. Get an aggressive doctor on your side."

"Both Dr. Braden and Dr. Brice agree on doing an FNA."

"Get another opinion."

So I can hear it all one more time?

"I don't want another opinion."

"You've got to take control of your life, Rell. You think you can have an FNA and everything will go away?"

"It isn't your call, Nate."

"You know they can miss it. One part of the node could be cancerous, and the spot they hit could be fine."

"I know," I said.

"Then why don't you do something about it?"

I was totally beaten down.

"I've got to go, Nate."

"Rell, you can't roll over on this."

"I can't deal with this, right now."

"Rell, this is important."

"Good-bye, Nate." I hung up.

I was doing the best I could.

CHAPTER NINETEEN

The next morning, my mother had to come in my room twice to get me up. I took a slow shower, and I got dressed even slower. I did everything I could to make us late for the FNA, but at seven a.m., I was lying on an examination table in the Pediatric Oncology Clinic of Honolulu General.

"Good morning, Estrella," Dr. Brice said. He was already masked, so I could only see his eyes.

"Good morning, Rell," Dr. Alaire said.

I smiled.

"Scoot up a bit for us, Rell," Dr. Alaire said.

I slid up toward the pillow. The green-paper top I had on caught on my jeans.

Dr. Alaire rolled a tray of instruments next to me. She pulled down a fluorescent light and aimed it at my neck. "You're going to have to take your necklace off, Rell."

"Can't I just move it out of the way?" I asked.

"Sorry," was the answer.

It was my fire agate, my magic stone from LB; I took it off and clenched it tight in my fist.

Dr. Brice leaned over me. He pulled the light even closer. I closed my eyes. "How are you feeling, Estrella?" he asked.

"Fine," I said.

"Good," he said. "It'll be over soon."

I heard him say to Dr. Alaire, "Here Carol, near the tattoo."

When I was in radiation treatment, my neck was tattooed with small dots that marked the corners of where I should get radiated.

"Got it?" He asked Dr. Alaire.

Faster the fiddle. Faster the drum.

"You're going to feel a little pressure, Rell," she said.

Let go the flute. Let go the drum.

"Almost done," she said.

I felt a tug. It felt like a rubber band stretching inside me, then there was a sting and some pressure. Then I heard them both exhale.

"It's over, Rell," Dr. Alaire said.

It was just starting for me.

When I got home, I slept until noon. I watched TV, ate some of Dad's pancakes, and went back to bed.

The results of the FNA wouldn't be ready for twenty-four hours. I hated waiting for test results. Waiting was the time you imagined the worst.

What's stronger? I asked myself. *Hope or fear?*

I heard the phone ring a few times, and Mom would tell the caller the same thing, "She's sleeping right now, but I'll tell her you called."

I didn't want to talk to anyone, not even Mom.

I closed my eyes. I drifted down through my bed, through the floor, into the fire.

About ten o'clock, Mom came in my room. "Mrs. O'Donnell called," she said.

I knew what she was going to tell me before she said it.

She sat on my bed, and held my hand. "LB died this afternoon."

We both knew it was coming.

"Okay," I said.

"Do you want me to sit with you a while?" Mom asked.

I shook my head. "I'm okay," I said.

"Just call if you need me."

"Okay."

I buried myself under the covers and curled myself into a tight ball.

Let go of the stars. Throw over the veil.

I gripped the fire agate. LB was dead. The next thought I had was that I could be next.

I replayed the intern's words in my head. "It feels suspicious." I wanted to rip that node right out of my neck. Just dig in there with my nails and get it.

This isn't fair. I had cancer already. I beat it. We had a deal. I'd go through treatment, and it wouldn't come back. It's not fair. Not now. Especially not now. Tess was dead. LB was dead. There was no one who could understand but Nate.

I called his house, but there was no answer. I tried his cell—I got his recording. Then I called Emi to find out where he was.

"What happened today?" she asked.

I knew she wanted to know about the FNA. "LB died," I said.

"I'm sorry, Rell. Do you want me to come over?"

"No, thanks," I said. "I called you to find out where Nate is."

"Oh, Nate." I could tell by the tone of her voice, she wasn't happy about that. She was going back to being herself, jealous of Nate.

"He's at Paul's brother's fraternity house," she said.

"I need to talk to him," I said.

"Can't you talk to me?"

"Not for this, Emi."

During all that time they spent together in the hospital waiting room, I doubted if he told Emi he had had cancer.

"Would you drive me over to the fraternity house?" I asked.

"I don't think it's a good idea, Rell."

"I have to see him, Emi."

"That place gets pretty wild," I said.

"Emi, I wouldn't ask if I didn't absolutely have to. Please, Emi."

"Okay," she said.

When my mother saw Emi at the house, and saw me out of bed and dressed up, she probably took it as a good sign.

"Emi and I are going for a ride," I told my mother.

"It's late, Rell," she said.

"We want to talk, Mom." I said it because I knew if I told her I was going to talk to Emi, she'd let me go out.

"Do you need any money?" she asked.

"We're just going to talk, Mom."

"Do you have your cell phone with you?"

"It's in my room."

"Take it," she said. It wasn't worth making an issue over, so I shoved it in my back pocket.

As we left, Emi said, "We'll be home in an hour, Mrs. DeMello."

I wasn't so sure.

The street the fraternity house was on was lined with cars. Music blasted from the house. Some guys were sitting on the front lawn, drinking.

"Are you sure you don't want me to go in with you?" Emi asked.

"I'll be okay."

"What if you need a ride home?" she asked.

"I'll call you," I said and got out of the car.

"Rell," Emi yelled from the car. "Are you sure?"

"I'm okay, Emi. Honest."

The living room of the fraternity house stunk with smoke. It was crowded with couples dancing, drinking, and lying on couches with their legs entwined.

I spotted Nate at the far end of the room, and zigzagged through dancing couples to get to him.

"What are you doing here?" he asked.

"I need to talk to you."

"Hi." A guy next to Nate, about six-three, with a shaved head, lifted his beer.

"Are the FNA results back?"

I shook my head. "Tomorrow."

"Then what are you here for?"

"I need to talk."

"You're the one who hung up on me yesterday. I guess you didn't want to talk then."

"I didn't want to fight with you," I said.

"Go home, Rell."

"Please, Nate."

"Look around, Rell." He waved his beer around. "Does this look like a place to talk?"

"Please."

"How'd you even know I was here?"

"Emi."

The shaved-head guy next to Nate was watching us. He had a copper goatee and blue eyes. I lowered my voice, so he couldn't hear me.

"You're the only person I can talk to. No one else. I need you."

"Everything is a crisis with you, Rell."

"Why are you being so mean to me?" The guy kept looking at me.

"Because I'm an asshole, remember?"

"I'm scared, Nate."

"Not scared enough." He jabbed the beer at me. "What good was that FNA?" he said. "They'll sit and wait and watch that thing, and in two months they'll end up taking it out."

"Maybe it'll go away," I said.

"Rell, you're still playing games."

He wasn't a doctor. He didn't know me. I wanted to scream at him, "Listen, you asshole, LB is dead!"

Instead, I said, "And you keep everything in your damn little boxes."

"I face things, Rell."

"No, you lock them away."

"Okay, you want to talk. Talk!"

It was too late. "Never mind," I said.

"Gladly," he said, and walked away.

The guy with the shaved-head walked up to me and offered me a beer. "You look like you could use this," he said.

I took it.

"I'm Keahi," he said. "The fire." He stroked his red goatee. "Nate and I play basketball together," he said. "But he never mentioned a girlfriend."

"I'm not his girlfriend," I said.

"So, what's 'not his girlfriend's' name?" he asked me.

"Estrella," I said. "It means star in Portuguese."

"So we have stars and fire," he said. "A good start."

"But everybody calls me Rell."

"Like Rell Sunn?"

Rell Sunn was a famous Hawaii surfer. She died of breast cancer. "In more ways than you can imagine," I said.

"Do you surf?" Keahi leaned over me, and put his hand on the wall behind me.

"I never even tried it." I saw Nate watching me.

"You certainly have the body for it," Keahi said.

Nate was close enough to hear him. "Go home, Rell," he said.

I took another sip of beer. "I'm talking to my new friend," I said.

Nate pulled the beer out of my had. "She's fifteen, Keahi."

"Relax, Nate," Keahi said. "One beer's not going to kill a fifteen-year old."

"That's right, Nate," I said. "It isn't beer that kills fifteen-year olds."

"I was just offering Rell some surfing lessons, a midnight swim." He shrugged. "You know I'd be a perfect gentleman."

Nate put his hand on my shoulder as if he were staking his claim on me. "Stay out of this, Keahi."

"Sorry, brah," Keahi said. "She said you weren't together."

I took Nate's hand off my shoulder. "We're not."

"Hey," Keahi said, holding his hands up as if he were surrendering. "I don't want to get in the middle of a domestic argument."

"I said I'm not with him. He thinks I play things too safe. Isn't that right, Nate? I'm afraid to face things." I turned to Keahi.

He nodded.

"Go," Nate said. "You deserve him."

Keahi snatched a six-pack off the table and tucked it under his arm. He took my hand and we ran down the street to his Camaro convertible.

Keahi popped two beers. We tapped the cans together and chugged them down. I felt a little sick.

Keahi pounded on his steering wheel. "Let's roll."

He sped down the quarry road, taking the curves tightly. I leaned into him. The radio blasted. I echoed his "Par-tee," screaming and drinking like I did it all the time.

We drove through the marsh, and I chugged another beer to Keahi's two.

"Have you ever shot the tunnel?" he asked.

I shook my head.

"A tunnel virgin!"

Keahi swerved up the Pali Road doing sixty.

"You ready, babe?" He reeled into the oncoming lane. He was headed into the tunnel—the wrong way!

There was a concrete wall on both sides of us.

Keahi blasted the horn, and the blare ricocheted off the walls. I braced my hand against the dashboard. I locked my elbows.

Oncoming car!

He hit the brakes. We fishtailed. We skidded and swerved. Keahi pounced on the accelerator. We were going sideways. The wall was right in front of me.

We spun and veered. Brakes squealed. Then the thud on to the road.

We were out of the tunnel, crossed two lanes of traffic, on our side of the road. There was more swerving. Brakes. We stopped in a cloud of smoke.

We were on gravel.

My hands were clamped to the dashboard.

Keahi threw his fists high over his head. "Yes!" He leaned over and stroked my face. "Rell, babe, you're not a tunnel virgin anymore." He slid over next to me.

"You almost killed us," I said.

He put his arm around me. "I gave you the ride of your life."

I could smell the beer on him, his sweat. I wanted out of the car.

He pulled me toward him.

"Don't."

He kissed my cheek. "It was just the intro, Rell."

"Let me out!"

"Relax, pretty girl." He kissed the back of my neck.

"Let me go." I pushed him away.

"You really are a tunnel virgin." He started to climb on top of me. "Keahi's gonna take care of that."

I reached behind myself. The door handle. Where was the door handle?

"Come on, babe. You're gonna love it."

The handle. I opened it and almost fell out of the car.

Keahi grabbed me.

"It's a good thing I was here," he said. He straddled me.

No.

He was grinding his hips into me.

I punched him.

"Relax, babe." He grabbed my hair and my wig fell off.

He stared at me, and I dug my nails into his face, then ran out of the car.

"There's nowhere to go, Rell," Keahi yelled from the car.

I scrambled up the hill.

"Come on down, Rell. We're wasting some good lovin' time." Keahi came after me.

I climbed faster.

"Come on, down, babe."

I kept running.

"Come out, come out wherever you are." He was singing.

I fell.

"I'll make you feel so good."

"Leave me alone," I yelled. "I called Nate."

"Yeah, you and Nate, cancer buddies. I got it now."

"He's on his way," I said.

"We'll be through before he gets here."

Dear God, help me.

"Shit!" I heard Keahi fall.

"I called the police," I said.

Keahi didn't answer.

"The police are coming."

I waited. "The police are coming," I repeated; but Keahi still didn't answer.

I stood as still as I could, listening for him—for his footsteps, anything. But the cars on the Pali were too loud. He could have been behind the rock in front of me and I wouldn't have heard him.

Maybe he's dead, I thought.

I climbed down the ledge, as carefully as I could. Then I saw him. He was limping down the hill.

Keahi got back in his car. I thought I was safe. I reached in my back pocket for my phone and called Nate, but he didn't answer.

"Hey, pretty girl," I heard Keahi call me. "Come on down," he said. "I'll take you home."

I called Nate again. I knew he could see it was me calling him. I knew it. He'll pick up, I told myself, but he didn't.

"Rell, just a ride home," Keahi yelled. "No lovin'. Honest."

I didn't want to call the police. If the police took me home, my parent would be beyond crazy.

"Your last chance, babe." Keahi started his car.

My phone rang; it was Nate.

"You would have loved it, babe," Keahi yelled.

Keahi drove away, and I crouched down behind a clump of bamboo and threw up.

When Nate pulled into the emergency lot, I saw him get out of the truck. I ran down the hill.

"Did he hurt you?" he grabbed my arms, pushed me away and looked at me.

"No." I was still shaking.

"Rell, did he do *anything* to you?"

I shook my head.

"Anything?"

"No. Nothing."

Nate held me.

"I'm sorry," I said, and sobbed.

Nate helped me into his truck, then he walked a few steps away. He picked my wig up off the ground, and slapped some of the dirt off it against his thigh. He got in the truck.

"I'm sorry," I said.

He handed me my wig.

"It was dumb, I know it."

"You were lucky this time."

He was right. I knew I could have been dead.

"You've got to clean up before I take you home," he said.

I saw my face reflected the car's windshield. My mascara was streaked, and my lipstick was smeared.

Nate stopped at Lanikai Beach House. The restrooms were open. When looked in the mirror, I was ashamed.

After I cleaned up, I walked over to Nate on the jetty. He was tossing pebbles into the ocean. I told him I was sorry again, but he didn't answer me. He didn't have to be so mean to me. I wanted him to know why I needed him so much, so I told him.

"LB died," I said.

He still didn't answer.

"It happened this afternoon."

"I'm sorry about that." He went back to tossing pebbles.

"Doesn't anything get to you?" I asked.

He looked at me. "Tonight," he said.

"I don't get you," I said.

"You want me to be afraid all the time?"

"No," I said. "I want you to *feel* something. To be a little out of control. Something," I said. "It's all so easy for you."

He stopped tossing the pebbles. "Rell, at the end of my treatment—seventy weeks of treatment—I had a full battery of tests. One of them came back with 'suspicious' results. It took a week of tests before they gave me a clean bill of health—after seventy weeks of treatment, there was a chance that none of it mattered, and I was going to die."

"What did you do?"

"I got stupid. I got beat up a lot," he said. "I picked fights with the biggest guys I could. I went down to the basketball court and looked for some guy to pummel, or for him to beat the crap out of me."

Emi's brother was right.

"Did it work?"

"I got beat up a lot."

I reached for his hand.

"Did anything work?"

"My grandmother called me. She said, 'Life isn't fair, Nathan. Life is.' That did it for me. Life is."

"That's not good enough for me," I said. "I want life to be perfect. I want guarantees."

I thought he was going to get angry and tell me to "move on," or "get over it," but he didn't.

"You got dealt a lousy hand, Rell. So did I," he said. "But what do you think LB would give to be in your shoes?"

CHAPTER TWENTY

The next morning, Mom, Dad, and I were sitting in Dr. Brice's office. Dr. Brice's report was brief. "There is no evidence of cancer," he said.

I didn't want to break the spell—no evidence of cancer.

"The node appears normal. We will watch it closely, but, given all the other information we have about Estrella, I'm confident that she will continue to do well."

"So the node is not cancer?" Dad needed guarantees, too.

"Mr. DeMello, unless we completely remove the node and biopsy it, I cannot say unequivocally that there is no cancer. What I can say is that a team of physicians reviewed Rell's case, and we all believe this to be a reactive node."

Mom cried. I cried. Dad thanked Dr. Brice and shook his hand.

If my life were a movie about cancer, it would have ended right there. The credits would have rolled by and there would have been a shift to a scene at the beach. Music would play, waves would lap, and there would be a wide-angle shot of me running barefoot in the sand.

I would have my face to the sun and my arms stretched over my head. A white silk scarf would billow in the breeze. The camera would pan out across the ocean, and at the end of the credits, there would be a still frame with the following words on the screen: "Estrella DeMello was cured of cancer."

But that's not how real life works.

In real life, I tried to forget that I ever had cancer, but it didn't work. I got angry, and crazy, and a little out of control. It took a long time for me to figure out that having cancer was part of me. It happened. I was fifteen.

I'm eighteen now. I'm sitting at Kailua Beach with Ajax. It's overcast and drizzling, and I'm sitting under an ironwood tree, watching the frigate birds soar. A few surfers are bobbing in the ocean, straddling their boards, waiting for the perfect wave. I want to tell them that there are no perfect waves, like there are no perfect days. There are only ordinary days—glorious, wonderful, shared, celebrated, and cherished miracles of ordinary days.

Acknowledgments

This story had many guides to shape it. My thanks go to Dr. Braden Alan Shoupe, pediatric oncologist, who shared his medical expertise with me. Dr. Shoupe treats his patients with hope, laughter, and prayers. Among the children he treated was my son.

My thanks go to Dr. Jeanne Hoffman, who counsels families with children with life-threatening disease. She read and reread this manuscript and offered suggestions. I want to thank all the nurses who helped me: Norma Meyer, Kim Kiakona, Jean Williams, and Sharlene Silva. And to my fellow librarians who encouraged me and checked my facts, especially Nina O'Donnell and Cindy Chow, thank you.

To Evelyn and Rick Maldonado, who shared their son, Nick, with the world for six short years, before he succumbed to neuroblastoma. To Patricia Bourgeois, a strong teen cancer survivor who is an author in her own right. Patricia and I emailed often during the year of writing this book. To Virginia Wageman, my mentor and first editor, who lost her battle with the brain-cancer dragon. To Toni DeMello, for the grace she showed in her final days with breast cancer. And to her daughter, Julie, for being the model on the cover of the first and second printing of this book.

There are others, who always stand by me. My readers, Charlie and Nicole Buckingham; my writing partner, Patricia Nelson. There are the gentle prodders and the firm believers in me: Mitsu Papayoanou, Caroline Spencer, Cathy Reynolds. And my mother, Anna Babcock, for her financial support in getting this project done.

My special thanks go to Corky Herbert, the teacher who nominated this book for a Best Books for Young Adults award. And to Rhonda Saki, for allowing me to read new manuscripts to her students.

I offer my thanks and gratitude to everyone who was part of this project. To Sumanth Prabhaker, I offer my thanks for his cover design and edit.

Lastly, to my husband Jack, my husband, my best friend, and a cancer dad who was nothing like David DeMello, Shantih.

www.ingramcontent.com/pod-product-compliance
Lightning Source LLC
Chambersburg PA
CBHW032255310726

48973CB00008B/2413